HYVILMA

Book 3 of the Kitra Saga

Gideon Marcus

Journey Press
journeypress.com

Vista, California
Journey Press

Journey Press
P.O. Box 1932
Vista, CA 92085
© Gideon Marcus, 2023

CREDITS
Interior art: © Lorelei Esther, 2023
Cover design: Sabrina Watts at Enchanted Ink Studio

First Printing February 2023

ISBN: 978-1-951320-24-9

Published in the United States of America

journeypress.com

To Xkylyr, who first plunged us into hyperspace.

Chapter 1

It's very hard to throw a surprise party for someone you live with. Especially when your house is a tiny spaceship in hyperspace.

I wrestled with the little response cubes I'd created with the Maker for the event. I still didn't have a real table in my cabin, so they were spread out on the bed. The cubes still kept lighting randomly instead of in sequence. I gave a few commands to my *sayar*, trying to fix the code. For a moment, I considered asking Fareedh to help. Pride won out. I'd already told him I could do it alone. Another run of the sequence. This time, they all lit up at the same time. I instinctively bit back a growl, even though it wouldn't have been heard through the hull metal.

If I'd had more time, I'd have been fine. But it was already B-Day, and I had another fifteen minutes at best. I had to laugh. After all we'd been through the last year, from the blind hyperspace jump of our first flight to the harrowing crash landing of our second, the most important thing in the universe was this current task.

We had to celebrate Marta's birthday.

Especially since we'd missed it—both of them. Her 20th imperial birthday, the one that used Earth years, was already 30 weeks passed. We'd also missed her 20th Vatan birthday, the one we'd have celebrated back home, by several days.

I might have missed it anyway. Birthdays aren't that big a deal for me. This time, I'd even had a good excuse: on the actual day, she and I had been on a balky space shuttle, scouting out a planet to make sure its atmosphere wouldn't kill the 10,000 refugees from Gloire we'd found in the *Émilie du Châtelet*, disabled in orbit after Jumping too close to the world.

But on our way down, Marta had made an off-hand comment about missing her birthday. I'd promised her I'd make sure it wasn't a complete loss. Now I was committed.

The trouble was arranging a party without tipping off the birthday girl, who lived less than five meters away. We had the time it would take to Jump to the system creatively named GM +84, where we'd have to stop to refuel since Hyvilma was too far away to get to in one trip.

I spent that time making a lot of *sayar* to *sayar* calls from my room. I can't cook for rocks, so I left that to Pinky. Fareedh has an artistic eye; I made him the Decorating Committee. Sirena — the princess, not the planet the grateful refugees had named after her — got to work on place settings since she had her own maker in her quarters. She assured me that they wouldn't get too damp even though her room was mostly swimming pool. That left me with the fireworks.

I'd thought we could finish the setup in the seven days we were in hyperspace. We didn't. Then everything had to be put on hold when we emerged back into normal space, GM +84 a bright orange ball in the dark sky. First things first: we had to find a place to fuel up. The water signature Marta had spotted from Sirena didn't come from a rocky world after all. It was actually from a frozen moon circling a giant gas planet. That meant landing, melting the ice, and converting the water into the hydrogen isotopes that powered our engine. All told, that was two days lost.

Fareedh finally finished his bit last night. Now that it was B-day, it was up to Peter to do the most important job: keep Marta occupied long enough for me to finish.

That part should have been easy. Marta is a sucker for physical attention. All Peter had to do was be extra affectionate this morning. Surely, I'd thought, Peter would have no trouble putting down his *sayar* and doing his boyfriendly duty. It certainly wasn't mine; Marta and I hadn't been a couple since high school.

It had been harder to arrange than I'd expected.

"I'm onto something," he'd said the other night in the wardroom, bleary eyed at 3 AM. "Maybe everything." He'd hardly been out of his room since we'd taken off, mostly leaving for meals and the gas-up operation. Ever since we'd found that crack in hyperspace, or whatever it was, inside the engine room of the wrecked colony ship that had been the *Émilie du Châtelet*, he'd been obsessed. At first, I'd thought it was just his natural cautiousness, wanting to make sure that torn bit of universe that had been *Émilie's* Jump Drive had really gotten destroyed when the ship crashed on Sirena. I should have recognized it was something else from the way his eyes glowed. The only thing that motivates Peter more than caution is curiosity.

I shook my head to clear it, focusing back on the stubborn cubes. Suddenly, it all made sense. Looking at the problem fresh, I saw what the issue was. A couple of edits later, and the cubes all lit in a row in perfect sequence. I felt my face broaden into a grin. It faltered as I bit my lip. Would six be enough? Was there time to add another one in?

The chime of my *sayar* caught my ear. A little holo of Pinky waving a green banner appeared above the device. Everything was ready. That settled the cube issue. I was out of time. Six cubes was the right number, I decided. One for each color.

I scooped up my *sayar* and the cubes and headed for the wardroom.

The *Majera's* wardroom was our main common space. It was where we had our meals, played games, held impromptu concerts—all the things one does to fight off the greatest danger one can encounter in hyperspace: boredom. Long and narrow, the room was the biggest compartment on the ship. Even then, it wasn't large. We'd made the compartment a bit more homey by painting the floor the color of grass and the ceiling sky green. It still could feel a little close, especially when all the seats around the big table were full.

It certainly didn't feel tight now. Fareedh had transformed the wardroom into a fairy garden. I couldn't make out the doors and walls anymore, or even the floor. Instead, the table seemed to float on a giant lily pad, and where the walls had been, the room seemed to extend several feet, bounded only by a low hedge topped by a vine-covered trellis. Only little ridges of stone, presumably holographic, marked where the walls actually started; Fareedh was smart to have included those, otherwise I'm sure one of us would smack their nose against a wall. Probably me.

It wasn't all holos and landscape wall sprawls, though. There were physical trimmings, too. Gossamer hangings in butterfly patterns were suspended from wooden poles. They fluttered gently in the…breeze? And on the table, a feast. I looked it over, swallowing hungrily. Three big serving bowls: pilaf, stew, a salad. And at least half a dozen kinds of pastries.

I must have stood there gaping for a full second.

"Do you like it?" Fareedh's low voice floated from the back, where the Maker and the food prep area had been hidden with what I thought was a gauzy mauve curtain. He stepped into view, materializing without parting the fabric. Another holo.

I stifled a laugh. He wore a brown silk jerkin, flowing from his neck to a wide silver belt. There was a short skirt, or maybe it was part of the top, and his long legs were in green tights. His dark, skinny arms were bare. A little red fez completed the ensemble. He looked like a Jinn or an elf or something.

"It's amazing," I said with a chuckle. "You look great, too."

He bowed with a flourish. Actually, the outfit did kind of suit him. The hose made his lean legs pretty cute. Fareedh wasn't all bones and knobby joints, thin as he was.

A pink tentacle emerged from the phantom curtain and encircled Fareedh around the waist. He let out a stifled little scream as it dragged him backward. As he vanished from view, Pinky's featureless hemisphere of a head appeared. He put another thin pseudopod to a place below the two dark spirals that were his eyespots and dramatically stage-whispered "ssshhh."

Whereupon Peter's brawny arm appeared, grabbing Pinky's head in a clinch. "She can't hear with the doors closed, *Pässi*."

The move in no way restricted Pinky's ability to speak, given that he could pump air through all of his body. "I am not a sheep, male or otherwise," he protested. "Anyway, she's due here any second. I just pinged her *sayar*."

"Eep," I squeaked, tossing my cubes on the table and heading toward the curtain with a pounce. There was just enough room in the cramped space to fit the four of us, though not for very long. I turned around, my back against the Maker.

"Why didn't you say that when you called me?" I hissed.

"And ruin the surprise?"

Fareedh whispered hoarsely, "The surprise is for her, not for us."

"Hmph. Surprises are for everyone." He folded his arms haughtily, shrinking a half-meter to escape Peter's grip. Peter looked like he was about to say something, but the gentle clunk of the wardroom door cut him off. We held our breath.

Marta walked in and immediately gave out a gratifying gasp. Her head swiveled from side to side, taking in Fareedh's handiwork. From this side, the holo-curtain was almost transparent, and I was suddenly afraid that she'd see us. That was silly, I told myself; it had been completely opaque from the other side.

I looked up at Peter. He nodded the go sign. I punched my *sayar* as we burst out from behind the curtain. A holographic rainbow of fireworks exploded from the cubes I'd set on the table, accompanied by our more-or-less synchronized shout of "Surprise!".

Which was almost, but not quite, drowned out by her shriek in response. She put a hand to her chest, startled, as little red and yellow sparks flew silently past her.

"Why…what's going on?"

"It's your birthday party!" Peter said, as if it was the most obvious of things.

"You scared me almost right out of my skin," she said, but she was smiling now.

Pinky strode forward on three stumpy legs to pat her shoulder. "Of course. Aging is scary. Feel the specter of death on your shoulder. You, all of…" He lowered his voice ominously. "Twenty. Years. Old."

Her eyes found mine, shining. "You remembered."

I felt my cheeks flush. "Of course I remembered."

She stepped past Pinky to wrap me in a hug. An embrace from Marta is no subtle thing. She's a head taller than me and much fuller in figure. And when she hugs, she does it without reservation. It used to make me a little uncomfortable, when we were going out, how often she'd find an excuse to do it. I felt a little smothered, I guess. Now… well, it didn't bother me anymore. My eyes closed as I returned the hug.

There was a loud coughing sound. "We were involved, too, you know," came Pinky's pained voice.

Marta let me go, hugging Pinky so tight that his middle got a distinct indentation. His rubbery skin deepened from his normal peony pink to a deep rose, an unmistakable sign of happiness. Then Marta gave both Fareedh and Peter a kiss, the first on the cheek, the second firmly on the lips. It went on longer than necessary for a simple thank you. I was almost jealous.

At last, she turned, looking quizzically over the still-sparkling cubes. "But where's Sirena?"

As if on cue, Sirena's voice rang from the far door of the wardroom. "Right here, darling!"

Her highness, Sirena Isabella de la Atlántida Jáimez, the Seventh, glided into the room, her egg-shaped grav chair just clearing the sides of the portal. She was no more dressed than she usually was, but the chain of opalescent shells that hung across her chest offset her brilliant red hair perfectly. We stepped around the table, giving the princess room to squeeze in close to Marta, who leaned over to give a thankful embrace. Sirena was delicate, almost fragile-looking compared to her. The princess' bronze skin had a glossy sheen, an inherited trait along with her slightly webbed fingers and the currently hidden tail, adaptations to her aquatic homeworld.

"I hate to invoke rank," Sirena said, looking up at Marta, "but I wanted to be the first to bestow a gift upon the birthday girl. I'm pretty sure these will suit you." She reached into her lap and presented a tiny box with the flourish of someone presenting a royal order.

Marta gently pressed it open, the top winking out of existence. Her eyes widened, and she let out a gasp. Her gaze flickered to Sirena's pointed ears, which were, unusually, completely naked.

"These…these aren't yours, are they?"

Sirena waved a hand negligently. "I'll get another pair when I get home. I saw how you appreciated them when we first met. I want someone of taste to enjoy them." She made a shooing gesture. "Put them on, darling!

Marta wasted no time tugging off her current pair of earrings and handing them to Peter, who had already sidled past me to take them. After placing Sirena's on her ears, she mirrored her *sayar* and held it up to her face. The iridescent half-moons, carved from an Atlántidan shellfish, suited her. Marta looked at Sirena, her crinkled eyes blinking.

"This is too much. Thank you." She turned to the rest of us, her face glowing above the slowly fading out cubes. "Thank you, all. I didn't expect…well, just…I don't know what to say."

Peter smiled broadly. "What's to say? Let's eat!"

Chapter 2

We ate, a lot. We talked about what we planned to do after we got to Hyvilma, and later, once we got back home. The conversation gradually wandered to deeper subjects. Marta was explaining to Sirena why birthdays were so important to her. Not just her, but those who shared her faith.

I'd heard it before. This time I listened.

It was the least I could do. I'd never pretended to understand Finitism. For Finitists, everything is part of a cosmic whole. Animals, plants, stars, stardust, Pinky's people, Bugs, even grilchies all make up this sort of universal consciousness. The coming into and going out of existence has a tinge of the miraculous, and birthdays commemorate creation. The idea of *everything* being connected, even aware to a degree, had never made sense to me. When Marta had tried to explain it, I'd shut her down. Worse, I'd felt justified. After all, *my* religion was state-sanctioned. Hers was on the "tolerated" list. And just barely.

Our diffence in faith hadn't been *the* thing that broke us up. I'd had a lot of rough edges. But it was a big one. Even then, she'd put up with me. *I'd* ended things. Lately, I was beginning to wonder why. Paying attention to what she was saying felt like I was making amends, in however small a way.

Marta finished her explanation with a quick uncertain glance at me. I smiled quickly and gave an encouraging nod, which seemed to surprise her. There was a moment of silence. Then, out of politeness, or maybe just pure curiosity, Sirena turned to Pinky and asked, "And you, darling? When is your birthday?"

Fareedh murmured, "Pinky was born? I thought he was radioactive bubblegum that gained sentience."

We laughed at that, but quiet quickly returned. It was a question we'd asked before, but the replies had never made a lot of sense.

At first Pinky did not respond, except to turn a slightly deeper shade of pink. I licked my lips, waiting.

"Every day is my birthday," he said at last. His eyespots slid to meet my gaze, "and you owe me a *lot* of presents."

"Nice try," I said, grinning. "How's this?" I wrapped him in a hug, his coarse skin warm and rubbery.

But Sirena pressed on, "Why is that, darling? Is it because you don't have days on your world? I've read that it is perpetually overcast?"

Pinky nodded, a strictly human expression he did for our benefit. "It's true. We didn't even know about the stars until humans came." He gestured with a pudgy hand in an arc above him. "But we always know when it is. Even with clouds, there is light and then dark. Every day is a new beginning." He paused a long moment, his skin shading to the maroon of puzzlement. "I can't tell you when I was born, because I've always been."

I leaned forward in my chair. We'd caught Pinky in a rare serious mood.

Sirena asked, "You mean you're immortal?"

"Oh, I hope not. You might get tired of my jokes."

Peter snorted. "Too late."

But the silence stretched, all of us still looking at Pinky. He could have deflected again, or maybe just made a big fart noise, and that would be that.

Instead, he went on, haltingly. "I remember a beginning. A dozen of us, maybe. We weren't pink but white." His voice shaded from his vibrant baritone to something flatter, empty of emotion. "It was a day when the smell was…" The word he used wasn't English or even human, more a kaleidoscope of notes. His skin tinged pale. "That is the first thing I remember. Someone's birth. Not mine, perhaps, but someone's."

Marta's forehead furrowed. "You mean you were watching another being born?"

"No." Pinky's tone remained inhuman. "It is my memory. But it was not me. It was…us." The last came out as almost a hiss, and a chill ran down my spine. Pinky normally went out of his way to mimic the humans he lived with, as much as he could, anyway, with a blobby body that could be any shape. He was my oldest friend, and until recently I'd never seen him like this, so alien. Yet this was the second time in just a few days he'd taken on this flat affect. It was scary.

As far as I know, Pinky can't read minds. But just as I was thinking that, his eyespots swiveled across the stump of his head to meet mine. Abruptly, he swelled and then quickly deflated. The resulting sound was a cross between a deflating balloon and a dying accordion. We all backed away instinctively, but no smell accompanied the display. This time.

"Too deep for me," Pinky said with a normal-sounding chuckle. "Remembering is hungry work. Pass me another baklava."

I stifled a sigh of relief, grabbing a sticky piece to hand it to him. I expected him to simply absorb the pastry into his pseudopod, as normal, but instead he made a show of pressing it into a mouth-shaped depression he'd made under his eyespots. After it had disappeared, he made a pretty good approximation of the sound of lips smacking. It was an elaborate display, all meant to say "I'm still here, guys. Don't worry."

I felt my shoulders untense, and there was a rustle as people repositioned themselves on seats.

"I'll brew some coffee," I said.

Chapter 3

We got pretty raucous after dinner. Maybe it was the coffee. I like it strong.

Pinky started the confetti war. He parked himself in front of the Maker and grew four arms. We had a better than even chance at taking him until Sirena took his side. For a skinny thing, she's got a serious throw. At least the princess didn't use her chair's shield to block our throws. That would have been truly unfair.

They had us under siege for a good five minutes. In between barrages, one of us would duck out from the table to get a shot off…and usually get showered for our trouble. Thankfully, the Maker was pretty low on goop after all we'd used for the banquet and decorations. Pinky reached into the thing, grasped empty air. That was our cue to rush him. Peter and Marta pinned his arms back, and I took a whole can full of the shredded paper and dumped it on Sirena's head. She shrieked with laughter.

We all did, even Pinky, with his weird guffaws that sounded like an accordion dying. If anything marked the conclusion of a successful party, it was that.

I wiped the tears from my eyes, my laughs fading to giggles. That's when I noticed we hadn't all joined the final rush.

"What are you looking at, Fareedh?" I had to say it twice before I caught his attention. Fareedh looked up at me from the other side of the table, brushing hair from his forehead. His ponytail had gotten undone in the chaos.

"Fusion burn. I think."

The words didn't even register at first. He popped up a *sayar* holo to illustrate. There was a series of abbreviations and symbols decorating a fuzzy photograph of what looked like a starfield.

"I don't...oh, I see it." A streak of light from a time-lapse shot. "You sure it's not a comet or something?"

"Yeah. It's not steady," he explained. "I've got the ship's sensors set to do an all-day sweep of the sky. I figured it was probably overkill given that this is a pretty worthless system. On the other hand, we didn't know that until we got here, so..."

"So you think another scout has showed up?" I asked.

Pinky stopped struggling. Peter swallowed his hiccoughing laughter and looked at Fareedh. "What's that again? There's another scout in the system?"

"Maybe." His tone was doubtful. "If it were a scout, you'd think they'd have left their drive on. This burn went on for just a minute. But when I tried to track the ship optically based on where it should be, I couldn't find it."

Sirena frowned. "Could it have Jumped out again?"

"He'd have seen that," Peter asserted. He got up to look over Fareedh's shoulder, putting a hand on the back of his chair.

Pinky peered, too, narrowing his head and extending his eyespots to just in front of the programmer's *sayar*, where there were more displays active. Fareedh looked down at the alien's eyespots, then up at Peter. "Do you mind?" he said softly, in amusement.

They withdrew and he continued. "That ship is still in the system, I'm sure of it. I just can't find it."

"Perhaps they've switched to thrusters," Pinky suggested.

Peter pursed his lips. "That wastes a lot of fuel. The only reason to do that is..."

"...if they don't *want* to be seen," Marta finished.

I frowned. GM +84 was a worthless system. A feeble star, an airless rock on the inner edge of its habitable zone, and a gas giant on its outside. The giant's moon was no prize, either. Outside, the poisonous atmosphere was just thick enough to maintain a pressure and temperature to sustain the few lakes of liquid water that would allow us to Jump back to Hyvilma. We hadn't even known about the water when we first saw this system on our charts back on Hyvilma. Otherwise, we might not have taken the long way around through Son Duryak and Purité to get to Sirena.

If there was another ship here, it could only mean a few things. They might, like us, be here to get fuel. They might be scouting it for the first time, hoping to find a good world to explore. Neither of those required stealth, nor did it make sense to blow their fuel using their antigravity to push them around.

There was only one type of ship that would not want to be seen, until it was too late.

"Pirates," I said out loud.

"*Por Dios*," Sirena whispered. Her face blanched.

Peter's eyes went wide. "We've got to kill the transponder!" He knocked over his chair lurching for the bridge. I was right on his heels.

Majera's bridge was a half-circle just roomy enough for five chairs in an arc. Sirena was the last one in, squeezing her chair in the center, flanked by Fareedh and Peter. The Window was on, right now showing what was actually in front of us. Wisps of orange cloud drifted across a dark blue sky. The giant that was the moon's primary hung over us, a sea-colored behemoth ringed with faint bands.

"It's off," Peter said. I didn't ask how he'd managed it. By law, the beacon that kept us from being a menace to navigation was supposed to be tamper-proof.

"We may be too late, though. Fareedh, how long was that ship in-system?"

Fareedh turned from his panel, pulling his hair back into a po-nytail. "No way to tell, though I imagine they turned off their drive when they spotted us."

"If we take off on thrusters, we'll be invisible, too, right?" Marta wanted to know.

"Sure, though it'll cut our Jump margin close," I said.

I cursed my luck. I'd thought I was killing three flies with one shot going to this new system instead of going back the way we'd gotten to Sirena. This way we'd get fuel, explore an unknown star, and avoid the fanatics who'd set up shop on the one good planet around GM +106, or as they'd named it, "Purité".

Well, it was what it was. I swiveled to face Peter. "How much fuel did we get?"

The engineer checked his panel, jaw muscles clenched. Then he blew out his breath, big shoulders untightening. "We're full. As of this morning."

"That's something, at least." I turned back to the Window, eyes narrowing at the dark sky. "They might be able to track us with their scopes, even if we don't use the engine. Plus, if we blow too much fuel on the take-off, we won't make it all the way back to Hyvilma." That system was at the edge of our three-parsec range.

There was silence for a moment. Then Pinky, sitting in the co-pilot spot, tapped recently grown fingers.

"If I may suggest something?" His tone was calm, though he had shaded an alarming faint ochre. I nodded, and he tapped a display into existence in the Window. It was a 3-D line drawing of the moon we were on and the gas giant planet it orbited. The other moons weren't in the schematic.

"Let's let Newton do the work for us," he explained. A slide of his fingers, and a curved line extended from *Majera's* position toward the giant. It looked like he planned for us to ram it.

"Is suicide part of the plan?" Sirena asked, her voice thin.

"My apologies, Your Highness," Pinky said, quickly rotating the display. I could see now that our path would not quite graze the giant, using its gravity to fling us out into space faster than either our engines or thrusters could. Once we got a safe distance from the planet, we could go into Jump.

"That's a tricky path," I said, rubbing the fingertips of my right hand together. "You sure we won't ram atmosphere at that height?"

"Provided Marta's measurements are right, we should be fine," he said.

I considered the course. It looked tough. We didn't know exactly where the planet's atmosphere ended. Come in too close and we'd have trouble. And it was mostly Pinky's job to make sure we got through safely.

"Are you up to this?" I asked.

Pinky slid his eyespots to face me. "I won't let you down," he said simply.

I felt something melt in me, right about chest level. Blinking a couple of times, I put my hand on one of his and nodded.

The Window switched back to all-visual, the bright, cratered ice plain stretching to jagged peaks on the horizon. Then we were looking beyond as *Majera* floated swiftly into the sky under the power of its antigrav. I pushed our acceleration to the edge of the compensators' ability to handle, and we were out of the wispy atmosphere in just a few minutes. I tried to watch three things at one: the fuel indicator; the constellation of ship's health indicators I called "The Tree"; and deep space. The last was mostly pointless. We'd feel a beam blast or projectile before we saw it, and Fareedh would see a missile's engine with his instruments before I saw it with my eyes. I could only hope our velocity would make us a tricky target. I couldn't wiggle us very much and keep us on Pinky's course at the same time.

"I wish we didn't have to fly blind," Peter muttered. "A few pings would light up whatever's out there."

"And give us away," Fareedh noted.

"I know, I know."

"I've got eyes open, don't worry."

But his calm words ended in a little gasp. I looked over my shoulder, and he was already looking at me.

"Incoming, Kitra!"

I gripped the flight sticks. "Is it them or a missile?"

"One sec."

There was still nothing I could see in the Window. Nothing but the looming bulk of the giant.

"It's too agile to be a ship," Fareedh said.

Sirena's voice rang out, "Why did we not see it until now?"

"I don't know. They couldn't have gotten a shot at us so quickly."

"Well, if you can see it, put it on the screen," I bit out.

A new display filled half the Window. Our course and something else's, on an intercept trajectory. It had come from the *planet.*

"A trap," Marta whispered. More loudly, she added, "They must have fired it into orbit while we were fueling up on the moon."

I felt Sirena's hand on the back of my chair. "Can we dodge it?" Her voice was brittle, the Spanish accent in her French stronger.

I eyeballed the course chart. The missile wasn't exactly following us. There was a steep angle between its trajectory and ours. That made sense. We'd taken off in a hurry, while their missile had probably just sat passively in orbit until it spotted us leaving. It was also on a continuous burn, trying to intercept us before we flew behind the giant. If it missed, it wouldn't get a second chance.

"What kind of acceleration does that thing have?" I called out.

I had time to wipe the sweat from my forehead before Peter answered, "30 gees."

Pinky whistled. It was about what I'd expected, though. A robot ship doesn't have to worry about crew comfort.

"We're going to have to let it get pretty close before I jink," I said. "I can't give it a chance to correct its course."

No one replied to that, but someone helpfully added a countdown to the course chart. Lord! Only thirty seconds. The thing was fast. I had to put maximum acceleration into the maneuver if we wanted a chance to dodge. My hands were clammy on the sticks, even as the handles did their best to wick the sweat away. I yawed the ship so our landing side was at a right angle to the missile's approach. When I fired the engine, I wanted as much deflection from its course as possible.

Ten seconds. It was now or never. I punched both the thrusters and pushed the fusion engine to full output. The antigrav made sure there was no feeling of acceleration, even with all that force, but the whole ship started to vibrate. The power plant pitched up from silence to a low, protesting whine. I couldn't keep this up for long.

My eyes were glued to the course display. *Majera's* trajectory slid sideways, edging closer to the giant. If we went on too long, we'd plow right into it. Maybe I should have pushed us the other way. But then we'd have lost some of the advantage Pinky was trying to give us with this course.

Five. Four. Three. Two. One.

The missile passed beyond us, missing by a good several kilometers. I heard a ragged chorus of sighs, mine the loudest of them. I flicked the thrusters and engine off. Now all I had to do was get us back on our original course.

Bright light flooded the Window before the dimmers could adjust. A second later, a sickening crash shook the ship. I was flung against my straps. All sensation of weight disappeared, and now only the straps were keeping me in my seat.

Chapter 4

"Great Infinity," Peter moaned. "They got the antigrav."

"What got us?" Sirena asked. "That wasn't a beam."

I looked at Fareedh, brushing aside my ponytail. It had whipped around in front of my face.

"The missile's off my eyes. I think it was proximity fused. It exploded close enough to hurt us without a direct hit."

My throat was dry. "How bad?"

Peter called up diagnostic screens at his station. I glanced at the Tree. My stomach lurched. When we'd taken off, the little lights had all been green. Now it looked like the gap-toothed grin of an eight-year-old.

"Drive's dead," he said, just as I spotted the browned-out light that told me the same thing. "Thrusters are offline, along with the whole antigrav system. The laser capacitor is out."

"Lord," I mouthed again. "What do we have left?"

"The power plant's working," Peter replied.

Marta added, "Life support is alright."

I tried to focus on what I should do next, say next. My mind was whirling. No Jump. No thrusters. No antigrav. Big planet. Pirate. Do something. Do *something*.

Pinky pointed at the Window, a finger extending toward our current flight path, which was now half the distance from the giant as before. "If there are no errors in the program, this is our primary concern."

I turned to face Fareedh. He didn't look at me, but after a moment of frantic tapping, sat back with a relieved exhale. "Ship's *sayar* just passed diagnostics."

Thank goodness. Everything was tied to that computer. I pounded the heel of my left hand into my thigh. The pain was something singular to focus on. I held up a finger to everyone, asking for silence, then closed my eyes. I could afford five seconds. Five seconds wouldn't be the end of the world, and if it was, nothing I could do in that short a time would matter anyway.

Deep breath, exhale, eyes opened. Now, one thing at a time.

We had about half an hour until we grazed the giant's atmosphere. Even with the antigrav off, we could still use the engines without too much trouble. We'd just be pressed into our seats. The issue was the pirate. If we didn't change course, and they knew where we were, they could plot our path and hit us with a beam.

On the other hand, why would they? I thought about it a moment. Then said, "Let's play dead for a few minutes."

"It's not really playing," Peter said. "What are you thinking?"

"If they're pirates, they'll want the ship intact. Ships are too precious to just blow up. I don't think that missile was ever meant to hit us."

"Unless they're just kill-happy," Peter shot back. "Maybe they're something like the grilchies."

"We'd already be dead, then," Fareedh said in a low voice. "They don't do subtle."

I nodded agreement. "They can see *Majera*. I want to be able to see them. If they want us, they're going to have to come and get us. Then we can evade. In the meantime, how much of our damage is repairable?"

Peter opened his mouth to say something, thought better of it, then turned to his panels. Tap tap tap. It was only a second or two, I'm sure, but it seemed to stretch interminably. "Fareedh," he said at last. "I think the antigrav's just on safety standby. It's stuck on my end, but I bet you can patch around it and use the backup subsystem."

Fareedh nodded, his little ponytail bobbing. "Yeah, I can try that."

"And the Drive?" I asked.

"I'll need a bit. I can't find an internal fault."

"What about the gun, darling? Can we fix the capacitor?" Sirena had put her hand on Peter's shoulder.

"You wanna shoot back? That's up to Kitra. Anyway, I think we're outclassed."

Pinky spoke up, "We don't know what we are. I can go examine the capacitor if you like."

"Do you have any idea what you'd be looking for?" Peter asked.

He shrugged. "I can at least tell you if it's there. And also inspect for physical damage."

"Let me do it," Marta said. "I've looked over Peter's shoulder enough times. If we have to move in a hurry, Kitra's going to need you."

I felt myself grabbing for her wrist. She turned, surprised.

"Wear a suit, okay?" I said.

She gave me a tense smile. "We've still got air pressure, but I take your point." She squeezed my fingers before kicking off and soaring out of the bridge.

It would take a few minutes for Marta to suit up and make her way down the lower deck passageway that serviced the Drive. All I could do was watch the Window. Silence stretched.

Abruptly, I heard Fareedh mutter, "Cocky bastard." I looked over at him. He added, "A burn, like you thought. Check it out."

The Window panned left, and a glowing orange circle highlighted what looked like just another star out of millions. But the spectrogram that popped up next to it left no doubt. No star would have that signature.

"Do we know how far away it is?" I asked.

"All I can do is guess. Can't tell if it's a big drive far away or a small drive close up."

"We can make a guess," Pinky said in that relaxed tone. "If we assume they're on an intercept course, then they have to take the planet's gravity into account." He examined his display and added, "Based on the angle of their burn, I'd say they're no more than 300,000 kilometers away."

Lord. Just one light second. Practically on top of us "You're sure they're heading straight toward us?" I asked.

Pinky rolled his eyespots over to me, "You know that's not how orbital mechanics works," he said drily. He was flushed slightly with amusement. I felt the heat of anger and irritation.

"But yes," he continued. "Actually, they are following us around the planet rather than trying to meet us on the other side. Which works to our advantage."

"How?" I demanded.

"Now that our ship is presumably dead, they are using the planet's gravity to slide in behind us so they can match orbital course and speed. If they went the other way, they'd whiz right past us. They could destroy us, but not capture us," he said.

I was starting to understand. "So we just need to get the planet between us and them." Sweat was a clammy chill along my arms. "It's a chance. We use the giant as a shield. Then when we're out of line of sight, hit the engines as hard as we can to widen our orbit and get to minimum Jump distance before they see us again."

"Assuming they do not hit us again before we leave their sight," Pinky said, his red tinge fading.

Peter barked, "Yeah, and if we can get our Jump online. And our antigrav, for that matter."

"Working on it," Fareedh said tersely.

"Antigrav's optional," I said. "We can take a few gees."

"Try sliding into Jump without it," Peter said with a grim smile. "You think you get sick now…"

Marta's voice came over the comms. "Just let me know when you're turning the gravity back on. I'm flying right now." There was a soft "oof" and the sound of magnetic boots clunking to the deck. "Okay, I'm at the capacitor. I'm unlocking the access panel now."

I rubbed my fingers together, waiting. In the distance, the little light inside the orange circle went out. Moments later, Pinky was already reporting, "I was within 10,000 kilometers in my estimates, and they are following us around the planet. We should be out of their sight for at least fifteen minutes."

"Is that enough?" Sirena asked.

The pause was longer this time. "I don't know." Another pause. "If they shoot at us, we'll have some extra seconds before their light beams hit us. Longer if they use missiles again." He looked at me with expressionless eyespots. "I recommend dodging."

I snorted. "Got it."

"We won't be shooting back," Marta commed. "The capacitor is burned out."

"Damn," I whispered. At the same time, I felt a touch of relief at a decision I wouldn't have to make. I had never shot at anyone before.

"No leaks here, by the way," Marta added. "Ship's airtight, as reported."

"All right," I called out. "Come on back, then."

Peter held out his hand. "Wait a minute. Love, could you cast your suit camera?"

"You don't trust me?" she teased.

"No, I just want to see something."

"Sure, one sec."

Peter's display sprouted a new view, a close-up of the open access panel.

"Can you lean back? Okay, stop there." He frowned. I couldn't tell what he was looking at, but his expression deepened into a scowl, and he muttered something in Finnish.

"Not good?" I said tentatively.

He looked at me, an oddly angry look on his face. "I thought it wasn't going to be a problem."

"...What?"

"See that brown line going up from the panel?"

I flicked my eyes over the screen a moment. "I guess?"

"The capacitor isn't in its original mount. It was so useful as a back-up Drive battery that I made a new socket for it," he said.

"Yeah, I know. I said that was fine. *You* said that was fine."

"Well, it's not," he said. His fists were balled. I was afraid he was going to lash out at his panels. He got a hold of himself, uncurling his fingers, but his face was still flushed. "I should have known. I was so damned clever." He looked down at his feet. "There's a reason warships don't integrate their weapons and engines systems so closely."

I swallowed. "Talk to me, Peter."

"The missile blast sent a disabling charge through our systems. It was probably meant to take out weapons capacitors. When ours went up, it fried the Drive interlink."

Fareedh looked up from his work. "Can't we just disconnect it?"

Peter shook his head. "It's not the capacitor. It's the burn damage. There's probably hairline char all around the Drive."

My heart dropped. Without a Drive, we were finished. Even if *Majera* could outrun the pirate, we'd be stuck in-system, and our food and air would eventually run out.

"Is the Drive itself damaged?" Pinky asked.

"No," Peter and Fareedh said at the same time. Fareedh gave a flicker of a smile, and Peter finished, "The ship's *sayar* reports no fault. The char around the Drive isn't the issue. The problem is, the char probably goes clear to the hull. Even a little patch on the exterior will be a problem when we go into Jump. The field might collapse — with us inside it."

Marta's voice came over the comms, "But if we can fix that, the Drive will still work?"

"I guess?" Peter answered without enthusiasm.

Sirena broke in quietly. "Which means someone will need to repair the damage." She looked up at the ceiling. "Out there."

I felt my lips purse. Fixing things in vacuum is tricky under the best of conditions. This close to a gas giant, there were additional hazards. Big planets often have deadly belts of radiation around them, solar particles trapped in the world's magnetic field. I turned to my panel and called up the environmental readings. Sure enough, the magnetic field we were in was strong, and the charged particles trapped in it would be lethal to a human in seconds, even in a suit.

"We can't do it," I said. "There's way too much radiation out there."

There was a rustle at the hatch to the bridge. It was Marta, undogging her helmet and letting the brown ringlets of her hair fly like little comets. "The whole way?" she asked.

Peter got her meaning and called up a display on the Window, a view of the gas giant and its system. Another moment, and now the giant planet was the center of a lopsided figure-eight traced in blue. The belts didn't go *around* the planet; they made twin loops that went out from one pole, around, and back to the other. Between the belt and the giant, the radiation was much lower.

"This is the radiation we mapped on our way to the moon," he explained. "Here's our current course." An orange line appeared, still grazing the edge of the planet.

Fareedh shifted in his seat. "We're going through the gap under the belt."

Pinky was already running pseudofingers over his panel, doing calculations. I waited.

"We'll have ten minutes in the gap, at least," he said.

Marta slid around Sirena to peer at the display, putting her hand on my seat. "Ten minutes would still be a lethal dose."

The hum of the bridge's ventilation fans grew loud in the silence.

"Lethal for a human," Pinky said flatly.

I whirled to face him. "You can't go out there!"

He raised his pseudopods in a very human shrug. "Someone has to."

Marta put her palm on Pinky's head. "You'll die, Pinky."

He turned an odd shade of vermillion. His voice, a mixture of fear and amusement, matched the tone. "I can expel the radiation as fast as it comes into me. "

"How do you know?" I demanded. "You've never done this before."

Now the orange tinge subsided entirely, leaving only Pinky's equivalent of a smile. "Have you ever seen me get a sunburn? Finally, a use for my superpower."

It wasn't funny. None of this was.

He stood up, taking Marta's hand and looking up at her. She was a good foot and a half taller than him. "It's just ten minutes. I should be alright. And it has to be done."

"It'll have to be done soon," Fareedh said. "We enter the safe zone in eight minutes." He looked apologetically at me. "Well, relatively safe."

"Then I'd better get suited up," Pinky said. His hand slithered off of Marta's.

"You better be back quick," I said to his retreating back. "I can't do this without you." I wasn't sure if I meant the maneuver or...everything.

He gave me a jaunty wave as he disappeared into the wardroom. I heard Peter say, "There goes the bravest gumdrop of them all."

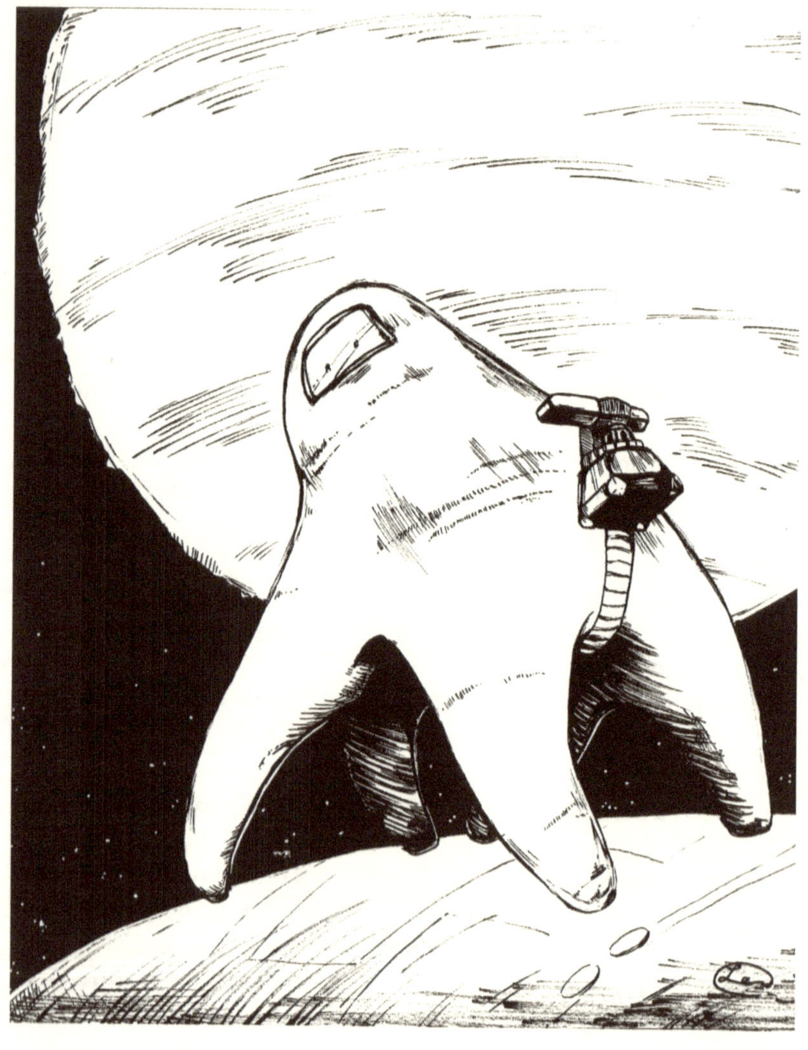

Chapter 5

"It *is* warm out here." Pinky's voice came over the comms, as clearly as if he were still on the bridge. I wished he were still on the bridge.

Marta whispered to me, her voice cracking slightly, "He's taking in almost a full sievert per minute."

"And me without my sunscreen," came the reply from outside. The pickup on our comms was sensitive.

"I'm making my way toward the aft of the ship. The giant is huge from here. You'll definitely want to fire the engines as soon as I'm back in. There's a course already laid in. I can help with the fine controls after."

"Just get to the char, you beach ball!" Peter called out.

"I'm going as fast as my five legs will take me."

A glowing red dot in the display inched across the edge of the ship, maddeningly slowly, while his suit camera view bobbed back and forth as one pseudopod after another moved ponderously on magnetized tips.

At last he said, "I'm here. The damage is pretty clear, but it doesn't look too bad. What do I do now?"

Peter, watching Pinky's display, answered immediately, "Use the atomizer. Put it on setting four."

"Rodger-dodger."

I could see the muscles working on Peter's face as he ground his jaw. His eyes were fixed to a schematic of the Drive and its web of connections inside the ship. His mouth parted slightly, then he called out, "You're doing something. I've got feedback along one of the points."

Pinky's voice answered, "The atomizer's working nicely. I'll have to use it on the wardroom table next time Kitra spills her nuclear coffee."

"Better than the essence of toxic waste you drink," I said, though my heart wasn't in it.

"Sticks and stones, Kitra. Sticks and stones."

I looked over at Marta's *sayar*. It read four sieverts already. I remembered reading somewhere that five sieverts had a 50/50 chance of killing a person inside a month.

Pinky's voice again: "I'm through the first side. The damage is a rough square."

"How much longer?" I asked Peter.

"At this rate, another three minutes."

"Can't he go any faster?"

"He's got to be thorough, Kitra. If he leaves any char, it's not going to help any of us."

I sat back in my chair, eyeing the real-time view of the planet we were headed toward. It was beautiful, a bright blue ball with subtle bands. Not at all like the drab Four back home in Vatan system, or the ugly brown brute of a world I'd had to dive *Majera* into to scoop fuel from its atmosphere on our first flight. But pretty or not, this giant was just as dangerous. I didn't want to go anywhere near its hurricane winds and planet-sized storms.

Pinky's dose was up to seven sieverts by the time he said he was done. A glance at the chronometer said only two minutes had passed, though it felt like much longer. Now his view was focused on the hatch he'd come out of, far down the bulk of the ship. He was moving more quickly than before. He must have been watching his radiation intake, too, or maybe he just wanted us to be able to course correct sooner rather than later.

Suddenly, Pinky's camera started bobbing about crazily, a blur of stars and pseudopods. He'd lost his grip! Sirena gasped, and her fingers clutched at my arm.

"Pinky!" I shouted.

The view arced from back to front, steadying on the hull of the ship. "I've got it. Just slipped. I'm almost there. Get ready to punch it on the heading I programmed as soon as I'm inside. I'll brace myself."

Another fifteen seconds. The longest in history. I poised my finger over the "execute" button.

A green light showed that the airlock had cycled. Almost at the same time, Pinky bellowed, "Hit it, Kitra!"

I did. The thrust of our engines pressed me into my seat, which contoured around me for maximum support. I'd only pushed it to one gee. Pinky may be soft, but he can bruise, same as anyone. Slowly, our trajectory started to change, deflecting outward from the planet's surface. Too slowly. We'd still hit thick enough air to bring us down or burn us up at the current rate.

I heard the odd rhythm of Pinky's pseudopods rustling in behind me. Then he was in the right seat, strapping himself in.

"I'm good," he said with force. "Take it up to three."

"Is everyone else secure?" I called out. I didn't take my eyes off the Window, the looming blue bulk of the planet visibly growing.

A chorus of affirmatives was the reply. I pushed the engines up, accelerating us at three times standard gravity. The pressure got a lot worse: a pain in my sinuses and an unsettled feeling in my gut. I'd pulled these kinds of gees before, even kind of enjoyed them, but this time around, it wasn't much fun. The strain of the situation mixed with the acceleration made my stomach churn. I belched acid, coughed painfully, and wished for the comfort of Sirena's grav chair. She was probably riding this all out just fine.

"We're doing it!" Pinky said excitedly. Sure enough, the curve of our course was getting more pronounced. We'd definitely miss the planet. But would we have enough time to get to Jump distance before the pirate saw us and could lock on? Ships that tried going into hyperspace too close to a planet ended up like the *Émilie*. Or worse.

"How are you feeling?" I heard someone ask. The voice was blurred by lips pressing against teeth.

If the gees had any effect on Pinky's breathing, it didn't show in his speech. "Just fine, Marta. I told you my people don't tan unless we want to."

"Are we going to make it?" That was definitely Fareedh who asked. He had the lowest voice of all of us. And it must have been Peter who answered. "I'm showing green on our Jump Drive now, but we're still less than half-way to the definite safe zone. Our tangent acceleration is just too low."

"How certain are you of where that boundary is?" Sirena's voice rang clearly over the rumble of the engines.

"I got a good estimate of the planet's mass while we were on the moon," Peter said. "My margin for error is pretty low."

"I can put her up to four," I said.

"Do it!" Peter's voice came out as a bellow.

Four gees felt twice as bad as three. But I was less worried about us than the ship. We were damaged, and we wouldn't know how bad until we got to a port of some kind.

"It won't matter even if we do eight," Pinky said with jarring calm. "Acceleration builds up over time. Our window is too short."

Sirena said, "Meaning we will be target plates to the pirates."

"Once they round the planet, yes," Pinky said. "We'll be in their line of sight in less than five minutes."

The roiling in my stomach got worse. Arms that were nearly three times too heavy trembled as I tried to keep my hands on the sticks. "Tell me when that happens, Pinky," I gasped. "I'll start to jink. At least we won't be an easy target for lasers."

Peter had overlaid the system map with the fuzzy circle that marked the safe Jumping distance from the giant. I looked at our course again. We were no longer in danger of hitting the giant. Now we had another problem. We'd been putting all our thrust into dodging the planet, trying to swing by as far above the cloudtops as possible. It was actually putting us into a wider, slower orbit. We'd never reach Jump distance in time this way.

"I'm going to push us straight forward," I said. "We should be using gravity rather than fighting it."

"Good call," Pinky said. "Sorry I didn't suggest it sooner."

There was a blessed moment of zero gee as I reoriented *Majera*. Then the engines were on again. If anything, it felt worse for having had a break.

A minute of roaring discomfort went by. I began to notice a strange feeling, like the ship had begun to vibrate. It was hard to tell if I was imagining it or if it was some subsonic rumble. I'd never run *Majera* completely without an antigrav, and the one time I'd flown a shuttle without compensators, there'd been no doubt something was wrong with that one.

"We're still not going to make it," Pinky called out. "The pirate is about to clear the planet."

"I'm open to suggestions!" I barked.

A fuzzy voice, Peter's, answered, "I've got an idea. I don't think you'll like it."

How Fareedh managed to chuckle, I don't know. "We have so many other options to choose from."

"Yeah." Peter gasped. "Kitra, I think I can get us into Jump early."

My instinct was to turn my head to look at him. Just starting the maneuver made stars shoot behind my eyes. I kept myself face front. "You're right. I don't like it."

"How is that even possible, darling?" Sirena said, her singsong tones jarringly unaffected by the crushing thrust.

"I've been studying that crack in hyperspace the past week and a half. I don't have time to give you the math behind it, but I think I can compensate for the planet's gravity well if I apply just the right power boost when we go into Jump."

"How did you figure this out, Peter?" Marta wanted to know.

"Fareedh helped," he said. "The *Émilie's* power consumption log gave the clue."

My hands tightened around the flight sticks. "Peter, that ship's *sayar* was as full of holes as Gruyére cheese."

"Some of the code was intact enough for analysis," Fareedh said.

I couldn't shake my head, so I settled on clicking my teeth with my tongue, the way Fareedh often said "no" without words. Facing the pirate meant probable death. Jumping from within a gravity well was certain death.

"Let's see what happens," I managed. "Maybe they're a lousy shot. Pinky, how much longer?"

"I'd start evasive maneuvers in twenty seconds."

The giant was receding now, though it still filled most of the port-side view. It'd take a second for the light of our drive to reach the pirate's eyes, another second for a laser to hit us. It would also take them a few seconds to plot our course. That lag might be enough for dodging, if I could make sure we weren't on that course once they'd determined it.

"Now, Kitra!"

Engines off. Yaw starboard. Fire. Hold for 20 seconds. Stop. Yaw to port. Fire. I was really regretting how much I'd eaten at the party now.

Two minutes of this. Then Fareedh shouted, "I've got another fusion flame behind us. Tracking. It's doing at least 30 gees."

"Ay Dios mío," Sirena whispered.

At least it wasn't a laser. They must have known they couldn't hit us, or maybe they just didn't *have* a laser. "Can we win this race?" I asked no one in particular.

Pinky answered simply, "No."

It got very cold. "How long have we got?"

"43 seconds."

"Kitra," Peter said, "We'll be about four fifths of the way there. Let me try this."

I got ready to do the next jink maneuver, then decided there was no point.

"Cut the engines," he went on, "I've already got the ship's *sayar* doing the calculations."

The light of the missile grew brighter as it sizzled toward us. Do nothing or Jump early. Both were suicide.

But Peter wouldn't commit suicide. The huge ex-wrestler hadn't gotten the childhood nickname "Mouse" for bravery. If *he* was advocating a choice…

"Okay, Peter," I conceded. "What have we got to lose?"

"Our lunch," Fareedh said drily. "Take your pills this time."

Engines off. Weightlessness after all that acceleration felt like falling. I jabbed at the console panel, got and swallowed two Jump sickness pills. They dissolved to minty mist before reaching my throat. My stomach settled almost immediately, leaving me strangely calm.

I swiveled to face the others, looking away from the missile that would now hit us in less than twenty seconds. Peter was working furiously at his panel. So was Pinky.

"Well," I said, "One way or another, it was nice knowing you."

"Fifteen seconds," Pinky said. "We'll want a margin if it's proximity fused." His voice was clipped, bare of emotion again.

"Got it in five," Peter said, his hands a blur.

Pinky raised a misshapen fist. "I've got a course laid in."

Peter was done, too. He paused, had time for one visible swallow, then stabbed at his console.

Pain lanced my belly. Even having taken the pills, the transition into hyperspace played hell with my insides, roiling them like the first few cramps I'd felt as an early teen before I got the shot that would keep me from menstruating. At the same time, the Window automatically went white, shielding us from the mind-searing weirdness of the sight of hyperspace. Nonsensically, I was still primed for the explosion of the missile. There was no way it could follow us into Jump, and even if it could, so far as I understood how hyperspace worked, we might as well be in entirely different universes.

No explosion came, of course. With an exhale, I pried my curled fingers from the grips of my chair and rubbed my belly, the pain already receding. It hadn't been so bad this time. Sirena let out a most un-noble belch, then looked as if surprised that it had come from inside her.

"Four out of five, Your Highness," Pinky said. His accompanying applause was muffled; his pseudopods weren't made for it.

Fareedh unstrapped and floated up out of his seat. Gripping his chair with one hand, he used his other to pat Peter on the shoulder. "We're alive. Good job."

The returning smile flashed broadly, then sickened. "We used a lot of fuel in our escape. I don't know if we have enough to get out of hyperspace."

Now it was positively chilly on the bridge. My mind raced. My first thought was to tap the laser capacitor for its energy. Then I remembered that there was no capacitor anymore. What was in our tanks was all we had.

"How much do we have left?" Marta asked. She floated to Peter's other side, nearly as graceful as Fareedh. Sirena drifted back to accommodate them.

Peter looked up at his screens, and his blue eyes widened. "That doesn't make any sense," he muttered. I turned and called up my own display. It said our tanks were 92% full.

"Okay, that's weird." Something must have been broken. My first thought was that it had to be the indicator. As my air-pilot friends back on Vatan used to say, "All fuel gauges lie."

Fareedh had seen it too. He was already back in his seat, running a diagnostic. "Confirmed," he said. "92%."

That was impossible. A three-parsec Jump should have used nearly half of our fuel to enter hyperspace, with the other half getting spent on the way out. "What were we at when we went into Jump?" I asked.

"93%," Peter said.

The princess asked doubtfully, "Are you sure we're actually in hyperspace?"

"I could turn on the Window to find out," Pinky offered in a deadpan voice.

"We…are," Peter said. "But these readings are weird."

"How weird?" I had visions of being trapped in Jump, food and air slowly running out even as our fuel tanks stayed full. A thousand years going by and our dead bodies dust in a still-living *Majera*.

My friend the engineer tried a smile, but it fit all wrong. "It's no big deal. I'd expect weirdness. The most important indicators are correct, and Pinky definitely fixed the hull." He chuckled weakly. "You've earned three bad puns."

Pinky somehow interlaced all three of his hands and made a decent approximation of knuckles cracking. "I've got some thinking to do." He unstrapped and floated up, steadying himself with a ceiling handhold. "Actually, I've got something else to do sooner than that, and I don't think you want me to do it here." He pulled himself up a touch to offer a cordial bow to Sirena, then jetted off through the door. I smiled. He'd taken on a pale blue tint, some kind of visual humor. I didn't quite get it, but I figured it would come to me in time.

"Well," I said with as much cheer as I could muster, "While he's gone, let's see if we can't nail down what all is broken and hopefully fixable on the ship. I don't want to be here longer than a week if we can help it…"

Chapter 6

Launch +67

When I was a kid, after my dad died, I remember three golden summers in a row when mom and I spent a week in a houseboat on Lake Bafa. My mother had a strict no-technology rule. You'd think that an ambassador of her rank would always have to be on call, but at the same time, that same rank allowed her to set hard limits on her private time.

So we'd laze in comfort within the wooden walls of the little ship, maybe forty feet long, just me and her. Once, I think, a friend from school came with us, but mostly I remember swimming under the wide green sky in the cool spring water, reading incessantly, and some of the best meals I'd ever eaten in my life.

This is how I'd envisioned time spent in hyperspace on the *Majera* before her first flight. Before I got my own ship, I'd been in Jump countless times before. But those were all aboard the ministerial ship mom took on trade and diplomatic missions to other planets. Time aboard was spent in regular classes and exercise sessions. It might as well have been a school with an indoor park...and no windows.

When I bought the *Majera*, with my eyes firmly on the stars, I knew there would be lots of downtime. It takes a week to go anywhere in Jump, a week of dead time. No dangers, not much maintenance. Nothing out there to see—nothing any prudent person should take a peek at, anyway.

So, with four friends on board, I figured it'd be the houseboat all over again, but even better. And being in Jump *had* been fun, sometimes.

Now was not one of those times.

Five days had passed since we'd left GM +84 and our fuel gauge read 91%. It wasn't broken instruments. A nearly full tank of compressed hydrogen isotopes masses more than an empty one. Even gross estimates using as simple a technique as banging on the tank's walls and listening to the quality of the thump told us we'd hardly used any gas going into Jump. I didn't know if that was a good or a bad thing, but it was different, and in space, different often means deadly.

I hardly saw Peter, Fareedh, or Pinky after the first two days. They were holed up in a makeshift lab they'd made out of the starboard cargo bay, running tests and making *sayar* models. It was clear early on that I had little to contribute. Marta and I hung out a bit. She kept up a brave face, but I caught her doing preventative maintenance on the air system, the kind one does when expecting a longer trip than planned. We didn't talk much about not making it out of the crazy Jump we were in, but it was never far from our minds.

Sirena did her best to cheer us up. Every morning, there was a new, inspirational phrase done in hand-lettered calligraphy stuck up in the wardroom. Yesterday's was 'The fishing's good in stormy waters.' Today, under a sign that said 'Full stomach, happy heart,' she treated us to chilaquiles. I don't know how she made those flatbread 'torteeyas' or got them so crisp, but they were delicious with the beans and salsa on top. But the smiles she got were weak and quick. Within 20 minutes, the wardroom was clear again. Even Pinky seemed to have lost his appetite, which takes doing.

Thankfully, Jump-out was just two days from now. We could make it, I thought.

There was an insistent scratching at my door. I looked up and blinked a moment. Then I remembered why I might hear that sound in hyperspace, light years from any cats. "Come in, Fareedh," I said, opening up the door with a practiced wave.

He'd let his hair down–the antigrav was working again–and it framed his dark features nicely. He was in a typical outfit: a t-shirt in muted rainbow pastels and tight knee-shorts. On his face, he wore a wide smile.

"Well, that's encouraging," I said. "Did you finally eat that canary?"

"Just about," Fareedh said with a chuckle. He very deliberately waited at the door until I pointed to my cabin's one chair. My heart melted a little bit at that. He'd been extra respectful these past couple of weeks, ever since I'd, as tactfully as I could manage, turned him down. I still felt bad about it. He's a good friend, as handsome as anything, and he'd even written a song for me. He was also, I had to admit, quite a good kisser. But when it came down to deciding, it just wasn't what I wanted. That he took it so well and was going out of his way to keep me from feeling uncomfortable, well…it was almost enough to make me reconsider.

"We think we've figured out what's up with the Drive," he was saying. I leaned forward, hands on my knees. He'd gotten my attention. "I did the modeling off Peter's data, but it was really Pinky's math that made sense of it. He thinks we've been doing Jump all wrong. For centuries."

I felt my eyebrows lift.

"Yeah, we've been hurling ourselves into hyperspace instead of gently sliding in. Actually, Pinky thinks we're not even technically in hyperspace, but in kind of an interface dimension."

"You lost me," I said.

He chuckled breathily, in genuine humor, not mocking. "I'm half-lost, myself. Okay, so the theory is that hyperspace is its own dimension, sort of a connecting layer with points that correspond to every meter of normal space. But for some reason, it takes less time to traverse."

I nodded. That was common knowledge.

"Basically," he went on, "Peter thinks that this isn't the case. Or rather, it is, but that there's more to it than that. He thinks that, when we go into Jump, we're actually blasting through the interface layer where the travel is done and ending up in some other universe for a week. Then we plow through the interface again on the way back. All of the real travel in hyperspace gets done in this sheet of overspace that's connected to regular space. It doesn't actually take a lot of energy to get in and out of it—only through it."

I frowned. Jump had been around for almost a thousand years. It didn't make sense that a bunch of kids in a relic of a ship could discover something all the scientists had missed. "How did no one figure this out?"

"To be fair, there haven't been a lot of examples like the *Émilie* to learn from." He grinned, eyes flashing. "Plus, Peter's a pretty bright guy."

I smiled at that. "A pain, but…no, I take that back. Peter's a changed man these days. He is a bright guy and a great guy. No qualifications." Fareedh nodded quietly, a sort of dreamy look in his eyes.

"Where is he, anyway? I'd think he'd want to deliver the news with you. Or is he still glued to his *sayar*?"

"He wanted to tell Pinky about the latest test, the one that confirmed his theory. The little guy went to sleep early."

"Pinky's not going to like getting woken up."

Fareedh shrugged, his gaze wandering over to my specimen table, the place I stored mementos. There was the coaster from Erkki's coffee shop on Vatan, the twin fossils Fareedh and Marta had given me on Hyvilma, the jagged lump of charcoal I'd taken from the edge of *Émilie's* crash site. But he was looking at the opalescent pebble from Jaiyk's seashore, the one we'd found together on our first trip.

He seemed to shake himself slightly, then met my eyes again. "Anyway, that's the good news. At least, it'll probably be good news."

"We'll know in two days," I said.

"I'm pretty confide…" Fareedh was cut off by a blare from my *sayar*. Peter's face appeared above the device, his features contorted with alarm.

"Everybody, quick. Come to Pinky's cabin. Something's wrong!"

Pinky's room was next to mine so we were there first. It was like walking into a fogbank. He'd turned the humidity up high, and the walls were pale, indistinct. He'd always been a minimalist, in his decoration and furnishings, but the emptiness of the room was extreme, even for him. In the middle of the small cabin, blurry with puffs of cloud, was a bright blue ball a little more than a meter across. Peter was kneeling next to it. He looked up at us with wide eyes.

"I've never seen him like this before." He looked beyond us, and we squeezed aside to let Marta in. Then we all backed against the walls so that Sirena's chair could fit inside.

"Can you help him?" Peter asked the princess. She was a doctor.

Sirena glided over to the balled body, dropping her chair and tilting it forward.

"I don't know anything about Pinky's kind," she said, turning to look at me. "Has this happened before?"

I felt my lips part, but my throat was shut tight. I'd known Pinky most of my life, seen him in every shape and color imaginable. But this was new, and clearly wrong. Tears stung my eyes, and I felt a sneeze come on, triggered by the moisture. It came, violently, but I could speak now.

"He goes into a ball when he sleeps. And when he's hurt, I think. How did you guys *not* notice this color?" My voice was sharp, accusatory.

Fareedh answered quickly, "He didn't look like this. If anything, he was more red than usual. Maybe he was covering it up."

"I..I'm sorry," I said. I should have noticed, too.

Marta, the only one of us besides Sirena with medical training, had her *sayar* out. She made a little "o" with her mouth, then said, "He's radioactive."

Peter took a step back. "Are you serious?"

"You'll be fine. Just don't touch him."

"Why didn't we check him after his trip outside?" I demanded.

"I *did*," she said. "He was fine. I mean, a little elevated, but it didn't seem dangerous."

Sirena was using instruments in her chair, reading displays that appeared above the rim. "She's right. These levels are quite high. I would wager it's concentrated at the surface. Pinky is trying to expel it from his body. Perhaps he has been trying this whole trip, disposing of it without telling us."

"Maybe we can sponge it off of him," Fareedh suggested.

Marta nodded. "Let me get gloves and some solvent." Sirena had to leave the room to let Marta out. In the ensuing silence, I became aware of a rhythmic rasping sound, rising slowly then falling more quickly. It happened in time with a trembling of Pinky's form. Breathing. Labored, agonized breathing.

Fareedh was saying, "It's a good thing this happened after we Jumped. There's no way I could set a course to account for distance, relative speeds, and all that stuff, like he can."

I glared at him, stunned. My friend, our friend was lying there dying, and Fareedh was talking about navigation. But when he met my gaze, his eyes were shining with tears. I realized he was just babbling, saying anything to fill the time.

The click of Marta's heels announced her return, and we stepped aside again. She had an armload of towels, and she got to work giving Pinky a methodical rub-down. Her hands were covered to the elbow with suit gloves. Half to herself, she said, "He told us he could process the radiation. He made it sound like it couldn't hurt him."

Have you ever seen me get a sunburn? I sniffled and wiped tears from my eyes. Stupid. His planet was *overcast* all the time. He never even saw the sun before he came to Vatan. But that didn't make sense. He never wore clothes. He must have had some way to protect himself.

"It's coming off," Marta said in a gust of relief. Then she frowned. "I don't know how much is left in him, though."

"I can do a quick model," Peter muttered, grasping for the *sayar* in his pocket.

Sirena was shaking her head, red tresses shimmering. "The damage is already done. We will need to…to…" She looked at me, dark eyes bleak. "With a human, we would give him a transfusion, culture new cells. But we don't have sufficient facilities on board for that. And I have no idea what we should do for him…"

"We need to get to Hyvilma," Marta said, not pausing in her work.

Fear was acid in my stomach. Would they even be able to treat him there? Hyvilma was the biggest Frontier colony, but it was still a backwater compared to Vatan, or even Punainen, its counterpart on the Coreward side of the Rift. Pinky was the first of his people to set foot there, as far as I knew.

I wasn't even convinced we could get out of Jump, Fareedh's hopes notwithstanding.

Don't borrow trouble, my mother's words rang in my head, almost as clearly as if she were there in the room. I became conscious of my fingers rubbing together, and I balled them into fists. I scoffed slightly. I was pretty sure our trouble account was already overdrawn.

Marta was half done with Pinky's sponge bath when he started to move. His eyespots migrated slowly from the top of his body to face me, and his bluish tinge purpled, then faded to lavender. Pseudopods struggled to expand from his spherical form. Both Sirena and Marta reached forward to stop him.

"Rest, my friend," Sirena said calmly.

"Yeah," said Peter in as light a tone as he could manage. "You don't need to put on a show for us. We got you." His last word ended in a swallowed choke.

Pinky wheezed, turning back into a ball. Then, all at once, his left side deflated with a loud raspberry. It was a matter of seconds before he was a hemisphere lying flat on the ground.

I opened my mouth to scream.

"Don't worry," Pinky gasped. "I'm all right."

There was a moment of panic as we looked at him and then each other.

Pinky, in a stronger voice, said, "All *right*. Get it?"

Marta let out an odd, loud snort. A laugh, I realized. It took me a moment, then I understood. I shook my head, wiping tears from my eyes, unable to restrain a smile.

With Pinky, comedy was life. And where there was life, there was hope.

Chapter 7

Launch +69

The bridge was an empty place without Pinky to my right. Yes, Peter and Marta were behind me. I could sense Fareedh, just out of my peripheral vision, and Sirena too, the occasional hum of her chair audible over the faint but ever-present mechanical song of the ventilators and machinery.

But Pinky's absence was like a hole in space. We were minutes from Jump-out without a navigator on hand, assuming we could even make the transition to normal space. And that was secondary to the idea that I might lose my best friend.

There was a jingling of bracelets, and thin fingers pressed lightly on my shoulder.

"I think he will be all right. He is no longer emitting radiation. I checked not twenty minutes ago." Sirena must have been reading my thoughts.

"But, he's still so blue." I shuddered at the memory. It was a bruised color, no longer uniform and bright. It was how I imagined an old corpse might look.

"He is trying to heal," she stressed. "I have seen the hospital on Hyvilma. It is extensive." Another squeeze. "Just concentrate on getting us there." The character of her voice changed as she turned to face Peter. "You, too, my engineer friend."

"I'm on it," he said tightly.

I gave Sirena's hand a pat, then scanned my panel. The Tree was an unsettling range of colors: amidst the reassuring green of the power plant and the life systems, there was a dead brown for the comm laser, an insecure yellow for the antigrav, an ominous orange flickering for the drive. Above the readouts, the Window remained opaque. What secrets did it hide? If we really were in some strange not-hyperspace, what might it look like? For a wild moment, I considered activating the display. This might be our only chance, if Peter couldn't replicate this Jump…or if we turned into atoms upon exiting.

My fingers halted halfway to the switch, as the memory of the last time I'd looked at hyperspace with the naked eye came back to me. The visions it had induced: a bizarre marriage of memory and fantasy that had put me in the seat of my glider in the middle of a hurricane, and then on the deck of my mother's ship moments before it exploded. If Marta hadn't turned off the Window then…

I shook my head. No. If we made it out of this Jump, then we could try it next time, under controlled circumstances, with safety measures. Like a scientific experiment should be. Not some half-cocked foolishness.

"How much longer?" I called out, my voice sharper than I'd intended. I could have looked it up myself. I just didn't want to be alone in these last minutes.

"83 seconds," Peter said after a pause. "I'm basically doing the same thing I did last time, powering up at the moment of egress."

I turned to my left, looking over Peter's broad shoulders to catch Marta's eye. "I don't know what traffic will be like. You'll want to check the comms for nearby transponders, and let the port know we've got a sick passenger."

Marta smiled at me softly, sympathetically, and nodded. I wasn't telling her anything she didn't know.

The odds of us running into other ships when we came out of Jump were vanishingly small, anyway. If Pinky had done his course plotting right, and there was no reason to believe he hadn't, we would emerge into normal space a good hundred thousand kilometers from Hyvilma, in the zone designated for arrivals in that particular hour. That frontier world didn't get too many arrivals, and in any event, space is really big.

I *still* worried about hitting something.

Nevertheless, I was already thinking past Jump-out to what would happen next. We had to get down on the surface as fast as possible, and any ships that got in our way, watch out! Our full tank of gas was actually a godsend. We could afford to be wasteful. I could zoom in at four gees, do a braking maneuver on the atmosphere, and screech to a thrusted stop in record time. Provided the antigrav held out.

My hands, already clammy with sweat, clutched at the sticks.

"Six seconds," Peter called out. "Better brace yourself."

Oh Lord. I'd forgotten to take pills. Did I have time? No, I did not. I gritted my teeth, girding myself for the transition. If it was anything like last time, it was going to hurt.

"Two. One. Egress." The last came out a hiss.

Nothing. No gut-wrench. No cramps. Astonishment quickly gave way to fear. We must not have left Jump!

Panicked words formed in my mouth, cut off abruptly as the Window came on, revealing a brilliant starfield. A small, violet-and-white globe of a world lay just to the right of center. Hyvilma, I recognized.

Fareedh was out of his chair, clapping Peter on the back. "That was beautiful, man. I didn't feel a thing!"

"I'm getting better at this," he replied with a hint of pride.

Sirena said wistfully, "With Jumps that smooth, even Consuelo might tolerate travel." I'd forgotten all about her, the princess' lifelong aide who'd been left behind on Hyvilma. She hadn't left much of an impression, though I remembered her being very efficient.

I turned to face Sirena. "Do you think she could help make plans? Maybe speed up Pinky's getting into the hospital?"

She considered. "That's not a bad idea. I'll have to see if we're in *sayar* range." She tapped the rim of her chair, and a phantom interface floated before her. I watched as she began the comm, then realized I'd completely forgotten about my collision worries. I swiveled, clutching for the controls.

"Are we clear, Marta?"

"I've got nothing in the immediate vicinity," her voice sang. "Picking up normal traff..ic."

I caught her hesitation. "What's up?"

"I thought traffic was normal. There are ships out there. Maybe more than usual. And there's a…I don't know…a hum. It's suffusing the commercial comm bands."

Sirena looked up at me from her *sayar* display. "I can't make a signal," she said.

Fareedh looked over her shoulder. "You mean we're out of range?"

"No. It simply won't send."

Marta's voice broke through. "I think we're being jammed."

"Us?" Peter yelped. "Specifically?"

"No, like I said, it's all across the spectrum. I don't think anyone can...hold it, there's one strong signal coming through on the Navy band. Let me tune it in."

I took a deep breath. If the Navy was involved, at least they might have a handle on what was going on. The Window lit up with a sensor display of the space around Hyvilma, the world fading into an outline. The planet didn't have a moon, so anything besides the world itself had to be artificial. Even without turning on our scanners, the display was speckled with dozens of lights, each with a little alphanumeric code next to them. Transponder codes. There were definitely more than I'd seen when we'd left the system, weeks before. And there was something curious about the pattern they were in. I bit my lips, contemplating. That was it: there were none close to the planet proper. It was like they were in some kind of holding pattern.

I remembered then that we'd left our transponder off after running away from the pirate. If the Navy was actively involved right now, that could get us in trouble. I turned to face Peter, since he was the only one who could turn it back on.

Marta distracted me. She had her hands over her ears, disbelief on her face. I caught her eye and looked the question at her. She set the comms from private to public. A strident voice filled the room:

"...say again, in the name of the Trans-Frontier People's Front, the volume of space within 30,000 kilometers of Hyvilma is controlled space. Any vessels who enter this zone will be fired upon. Further instructions will be provided within the next twelve hours. I say again, in the name of..."

Marta turned off the comms and spread out her hands in an expression of confusion. "It just repeats."

"Who are these people?" Sirena asked.

"No clue," I said. "No, wait." I cast my mind back. There was a dim memory from...fifth grade? Mom meeting with a representative from a group. It wasn't a planetary leader. "Yeah, the FPTF. I remember a friend and I thought it was the funniest name ever, like the sound of people spitting at each other. They shouldn't be here, though. The FPTF was on Sennet and Talvi."

"And now," Sirena said matter-of-factly, "they are here."

I looked at Fareedh. "That doesn't make any sense. There's a giant cruiser standing guard over the planet making sure no one messes with the Trans-Rift ferry. The *Faucon*. Your brother's on board, you said."

His eyebrow rose. "He is at that."

"Folks," Marta said. "You're not going to like this."

"As opposed to all the other things we have to like at this moment," Peter said.

"What is it, darling?"

Marta looked bleakly at Sirena. "The message is coming *from* the *Faucon*."

"We're dead," Fareedh said, his voice so low as to be almost inaudible.

"Are you sure, Marta?" the princess asked. "Maybe it's coming from behind the cruiser? On the surface, perhaps?"

Marta's lip quirked, and she put a hand on her hip. "A sphere's only got one center, and this was a broadband comm. Here, I'll show you." She turned to her panel, and a red circle enclosed one of the dots. All the other dots had given it a wide berth. We were actually the closest ship to it.

"So we've got about 20,000 tons of cruiser calling the shots out there," Peter observed.

Fareedh added, "Making sure no one gets in or out of the Frontier."

"This end of it, anyway," Marta noted. "With Hyvilma blockaded, no one can get fuel to Jump out and warn someone."

"Hey!" Peter cried. "Except us! We've got plenty of fuel. We don't even need the ferry. We can make it all the way across the Rift back to Punnainen on our own. They'll never even know we were here."

I didn't say anything. "What?" he said, flushing under my glare. Then his grin faded as quickly as it had grown. "Oh, right."

"Yeah, right." I said. "Pinky might not last the trip back. And anyway, he's the only one who could plot that course."

"So we've got to get down to the planet, one way or another." Sirena eyed the screen, contemplating. "Perhaps we could sneak past him. The *Faucon*, I mean."

I thought about it. If I could trust the thrusters, and if the cruiser hadn't seen us pop in, we could maybe slide in without a burn. Especially if we planned our orbit so the big ship was always on the other side of the world. Except that we'd come out of hyperspace right next to the thing, comparatively. There was no real way to use Hyvilma as a shield. And even without using our drive, we wouldn't be invisible. Just less obvious than a ship with its fusion flame going.

"It'd be tricky," I said. "And if the rebels have taken the planet, or even just the capital, it won't do us any good."

Marta said, "There's nothing on the city bands. No broadcasts, nothing on the *sayar* relay channels. I can't tell what's going on down there except that it's not business as usual."

"That's because it's being blocked by the jamming, yeah?" Fareedh asked.

She frowned, shaking her head. "I'd still know if there were transmissions even if I couldn't decipher them. Anyway, the jamming is just on normal space frequencies. It wouldn't interfere with the ones in use on the planet."

Peter folded his arms. "I think we gotta assume they've taken the city."

"We can't even ask the rebels for help, what with them jamming our comms," I said. It came out almost as a whine. My fingers twitched. Pinky needed help *now*.

Fareedh sat back in his chair deliberately, crossing one leg over the other. He had a faraway look on his face. "You said they're not jamming all of the frequencies, right, Marta?"

"That's right. Just the standard space ones."

"And we're how far from the *Faucon*?"

"1000 kilometers. Well, 987. We're getting closer, but we're not heading right toward them."

I looked hopefully at Fareedh. "You've got an idea."

His eyes widened ever so slightly in reply. "We'll want to be closer, though."

"I don't like this idea," Peter said.

Sirena laughed softly. "I imagine he can shoot us at considerably greater ranges than where we are now. What is the plan, my friend?"

"Iskender's on that ship. If we can get close enough, I can use my *sayar* to contact him."

"Won't that give us away?" I asked. "They'll hear us."

He smiled enigmatically. "Not with our setup." His mirth faded away. "Of course, I don't know if he's around to answer. Or what he can do if he is."

"Don't borrow trouble," Sirena and I said at the same time. She gave me a quick flash of a grin.

Marta spoke up, "How close do you need to get? *Sayar* range is a few kilometers, at best, without a relay network."

The idea of getting that close to the *Faucon* made my scalp itch.

"Can't you just use normal ship's comms?" I asked. "Plug your *sayar* into the ship's *sayar*?"

"Oh. Duh."

I exhaled a little laugh. "You just left that there for me to figure out so I'd look like the smart one."

"That's right. Well, it will be a bit of a pain. I'll have to transfer the program and I'll need help calibrating to *Majera's* power and gain. But I could get it done in…half an hour? With Marta's help?"

A half an hour sounded like a very long time. We'd Jumped into the area of space reserved for that time's arrivals. The *Faucon* had to be watching the area. It was only a matter of time before they spotted us, even without the transponder. A new, unwinking star in the sky, drifting against a black background.

That gave me an idea.

"I'm going to tumble the ship," I said. "Maybe they'll think we're a stray meteor or something." I nodded to Fareedh. "Go ahead and do what you have to do. I don't have any other ideas, so we might as well do the one thing we can."

Fareedh nodded to me, then looked over at Marta. "Let's do it in the wardroom. We can spread out on the table." They left, leaving the door open. Before I'd swiveled back toward the Window, they'd already tossed out a half dozen displays and begun an animated conversation.

A quick bit of thrust sent *Majera* spinning on all three axes. The stars began drifting in lazy, irregular spirals. Our ship, just two hundred tons in mass, was about the smallest an interstellar vessel could be. I could only hope we were too little to be noticed. If not, I hoped the rebels would at least have the courtesy to comm us before shooting. I didn't even want to think about the kind of ways such a huge ship could destroy us before we even knew we were being shot at.

I rubbed my eyes. "We were gone, what, 40 days?" I asked no one in particular.

"It does seem that events have moved rather quickly," Sirena said. I reached over to Pinky's panel and collapsed his seat. The memory plastic flattened into the deck, making room for Sirena to drift next to me. She nodded at the courtesy, rotated to face me, and laced delicate fingers in her lap.

"What else do you know about the, ah, FPTF?"

My shrug went all the way up to my eyebrows. "Nothing, really. I was just a kid when mom was doing her thing. Politics was a bunch of boring ceremonies and waiting for her to get out of meetings that went on for days."

"I think I've got something. There was a thing about them in the news before we left Vatan," Peter said. He moved over to Fareedh's seat, swapping displays. This way, he wasn't behind me. He went through his *sayar* a moment, then called up an article with some embedded holo of about a dozen dressed-up people around a table. Peter started to read in an untrained monotone, "'Talvi Conference outlines new goals, touts new members. Meeting for an unprecedented third time, the Frontier Rights Group, the political arm of the separatist Trans-Frontier People's Front, announced that they had opened up offices on Syr Darya and Hyvilma with the ultimate goal of increasing the number of delegates in the Sennetian parliament. Their stated hope was to establish a kingmaking minority such that the ensuing ruling coalition would send a more autonomy-minded representative to the Core.' His eyes flicked further down the piece. "Stuff, stuff, stuff. Conference chancellor Fatime Berisha enthusiastic about upcoming elections. Stuff and stuff. Famine relief sub-agency created. Stuff. Stuff. 'Important that the Empire not repeat the needless mistakes that characterized its annexation of the Midworlds,' Berisha said…"

I looked up automatically at Sirena, feeling myself flush. Atlán-tida was a Midworld. They still got short shrift. Senior history class had spent a good four weeks on the Imperial constitution, but sort of glossed over the bit after Jump 3 was developed and the Empire conquered its way from the Core to the Rift. Marta was a Midworlder, too, sort of. She traced lineage on both sides back to Ääreẗtömyys, the smashed home of Finitism. Hers and Peter's view of the Crown was…less than charitable.

There was a reason I tried to stay out of politics. What was past was past, and anyway, mom had been an Imperial ambassador, ranked above provincial cabinet members. She *was* the government, so far as I was concerned. I couldn't see her working for an evil organization.

And yet, here I was, cheeks red.

But Sirena was looking at Peter. "That doesn't sound like a mani-festo," she said.

"No," he said. "Pretty typical stuff. I only remember it because I've got the politics column at the top of my feed and the name Berisha was unusual."

I stuck out my tongue. "I didn't know you followed politics."

"I don't *just* fix things," he said. "And it's better than sports. It actually means something."

Sirena chuckled. "Don't let my cousins hear you say that. They take polo very seriously." She sobered quickly. "Is it possible that this is all a ruse? A, how you say, disguise for something more prosaic?"

"You mean, like, a hijacking?" I asked.

"Who knows?"

I stole a glance at the Window. The red-circled star that was the *Faucon* spiraled leisurely into view. I honestly didn't know which op-tion was worse: a frontier-wide civil war or a gang of pirates so skilled they could take over a Navy ship.

"Either way, we have to deal with that ship before we can get help for Pinky," I said, my voice faltering on my friend's name.

Chapter 8

A loud "Got it!" from the wardroom preceded the sound of sandaled and heeled feet running back onto the bridge. It had been just 18 minutes.

"That was quick," Peter said, giving Fareedh a little embarrassed smile as he vacated his seat.

"Marta's good at her job," Fareedh said simply, sitting down.

Marta wrinkled her nose prettily. "Bio's half *sayar* science. All the modeling."

Peter offered Marta his hand. She took it and squeezed.

"So, what do we do?" I asked. "Just…call him up?"

Marta nodded. "Fareedh's channel is slow, text-only. It mimics cosmic radio noise, with the information on a tight subfrequency." She wrung her hands. "I just wish the laser were working."

"Why's that, darling?" Sirena asked.

"Our comms go out in all directions. If it gets picked up in multiple places, like, say, the *Faucon* and a ground base, or another rebel ship we don't know about, they'll know the signal's origin is local."

Peter's jaw worked a moment. "How close are we?" he asked.

"832 km."

"That's pretty close. The planet's tens of thousands of kilometers away, and the nearest ships are not much closer. Just comm at low power. The signal might not even make it through the atmosphere," he said.

Her smile was warmth itself. "I knew I kept you around for a reason."

"Well, shucks…"

They looked at each other for what seemed an age. I felt my fingers twitching. "The sooner we call, the sooner we can figure out what's going on," I said.

"Right," Marta said, her cheeks coloring. "Fareedh? Makes sense for you to send the message."

"I'll start simple. 'What the hell is going on?'"

Sirena asked suddenly, "That won't get him in trouble, will it? Getting a message? If he is under guard, say."

Fareedh shook his head. "We programmed our *sayars* for subvocal alerts on this channel. No one will notice." His Adam's apple went up and down, once. "At least, I hope so."

He turned and tapped at his console. It took just a few seconds.

"That's that," he said after a heavy sigh. He looked over his shoulder at me. "There's no telling how long it'll take for him to reply or even see the message. His *sayar* might be off or locked up or..."

A chime from his panel cut him off.

"Well that was quick," he said.

Peter got up to look over Fareedh's shoulder. "What's it say?"

"'Five minutes.'"

"That's it?" I asked.

Bony shoulders shrugged. "That's it. Maybe he wants to get somewhere private." Worry and relief fought momentarily across Fareedh's features. They compromised at anxious neutrality.

My heart pulsed in my ears. At least Iskender was alive. I hoped so, anyway. If we'd just given ourselves away...

It was a long five minutes.

We all jumped at the sound of the comm ping. This time, Fareedh spent a good while reading over the transmission. He threw it to our panels when he was done. It read:

"*Tolga. Where are you? You must be close. In which case, be very careful. I am holed up in aft section, Deck 4, with 6 other crew. Mutineers are on the bridge. They vaporized two ships that tried to make a run for it. Captain and first officer dead. Over.*"

I blew out a breath between closed lips, making a popping sound.

"Yeah," Fareedh agreed. "Not great."

"What does Tolga mean?" Sirena asked.

Fareedh smiled. "Means it's Iskender talking. No one else would get it."

Peter gripped Fareedh's shoulder. "We have to reply."

"What do I say?"

I tried to imagine the tactical situation. If some of the crew was free, the rebels couldn't have full control. It didn't sound like Iskender was under guard. "Ask him if the rebels have the whole ship," I said. "How long has this been going on? Are there other ships involved?"

"Okay, just a sec."

I watched the chronometer mark each moment. The response took 67 seconds to arrive, popping up on all our displays at once.

"Don't know current status of ship. Rebels must have substantial control to operate arms and engines. There could be other loyalists. Mutiny happened 12 hours ago. No one's searched our hidey hole yet. Don't know how far rebellion goes. No signs of other ships involved. Can you get help? Over."

"Tell him we can't leave," I said. "We've got a sick person who'll die without treatment. And we're too close to the *Faucon,* anyway. Ask him what he plans to do."

This time, we got a reply just 43 seconds later.

"If it stays quiet, we'll try to find more friends. Have sidearms."

"How many people are on the *Faucon?*" Sirena wanted to know.

Marta answered, "At least 200."

Peter said. "Seven against 200? That's lousy odds."

But Iskender wasn't through. Maybe he'd had to think hard about sending the next message. It read simply:

"Can you help? Over."

Fareedh rubbed his eyes. "Oh boy."

I looked over at Fareedh. He was frowning darkly at the message.

"We can't," Peter said quickly.

Fareedh didn't reply. His mouth worked soundlessly. He turned to me, moistened his lips.

"Can't we?" he asked. It was barely more than a whisper.

"Are you serious?" That was me and Peter at the same time.

Peter went on, "That's ludicrous. You heard what that cruiser did to ships that tried to get away. Imagine what they'll do to us if we try getting *closer.* And then how do we get on board? Once we're on board, how are we supposed to help?"

Fareedh wasn't looking at Peter. He was looking at me, as if I had all the answers. All I knew was that my best friend was dying, Fareedh's brother was in danger…and there was nothing we could do.

"You frame the problem elegantly," Sirena said crisply. "Yes, darling, most elegantly." Her chair whirred faintly as it rose a few inches from the floor. "If we are to help, we have three hurdles to overcome. If it be impossible to surmount any of the three, then I suppose we can remain tumbling in space until the situation resolves itself, one way or the other."

Her dark eyes flashed. "I am not accustomed to simply waiting things out, however."

There was a rustle of skirts as Marta uncrossed her legs and leaned forward. "We've got the beamers we took from the Puritans," she said.

Lord. She wanted to go in, guns blazing. I shuddered in a sudden chill.

Peter's huge hands clenched, opened again. "Are you loony? We're not soldiers!"

"I'm just saying we're not unarmed," Marta said calmly. She stood, almost two meters tall, eye to eye with Peter. In the moment, it seemed she could plow through duralloy.

"How are we supposed to get on board?" Peter's voice rose half an octave. "If we change course to make for them, they'll know we're here. And even if we close the distance, how do we get inside?"

There was no immediate answer to that. Half of me recoiled from such a foolish idea. Not just that we might get killed, but that we might have to hurt other people. With guns. Lord, what in the world could prepare me for that?

My other half screamed louder: Pinky was dying. Do *something*. There was no way to get down to the planet as is. The *Faucon*'s sick bay was the only medical facility we could conceivably get to.

An image of the crippled *Émilie du Châtelet* flashed across my mind. Fareedh tapping his console, and the colony ship's doors, previously unresponsive, opening to let us in.

I was standing before I realized I'd taken to my feet.

"Fareedh, could you tap into the *Faucon*'s ship's *sayar*?" I said in a rush.

Dark eyes widened in a quick flash, wheels turning behind them. He nodded slowly.

"There's security. It's not like the *Émilie*." His tone was musing, not negative.

Sirena spoke up, "You think Iskender can get you through that security, do you not?"

"Yeah." Fareedh nodded again, and the ghost of a smile appeared on his face. "Yeah. If he's out and about, he could get into a hard access point. They wouldn't even know he's in the system."

"And then?" I asked. I had a vague idea of him turning off the cruiser's guns, maybe even the lights. *That* would cause confusion.

He shrugged. "No clue. I don't break into Navy systems." He added, "…often."

I snorted a tiny laugh. "How many times have you broken into Navy systems?"

"Three," he said, flashing white teeth.

I shook my head, a smile forming on my lips. I looked at Peter, whose fair face had gone almost white.

"Peter," I said tentatively. "This isn't a dictatorship. It's not even a democracy. It's just us, all of us. I won't force you to do anything you…you can't do."

He stiffened at that, color rushing to his cheeks. He stared at me a moment, turned his gaze to Fareedh, then back to the door and through it, to Pinky's door, before returning his gaze to mine. He reached out for Marta's hand, like clutching a hold against weightlessness. She squeezed.

"Things happen for a reason," Peter said slowly. "We're here, at the right place, and the right time."

He took a deep breath. "I'm in."

Chapter 9

"Going to sneak through auxiliary passage to hardpoint. Hopefully unguard-ed. Have hooked sayar *to vitals. If shot, you'll know when I do. Out."*

I blew out my breath. That was as ominous a message as could be. I eyed the narrow length of the *Faucon* warily, now close enough to be more than a speck at full magnification. We were reaching the closest our orbits would take us, about 500 kilometers, before our respective paths took us further apart. I wanted to get moving sooner rather than later, to minimize the chance of our discovery. But there was literally nothing we could do until Iskender was in position.

Something growled behind me. Startled, I swung around, only to find Peter with a fist to his stomach, an embarrassed smile on his face.

"You're hungry?" I said incredulously.

He shook his head. "Opposite problem. Think you can excuse me a moment?"

Fareedh chuckled. "Better take care of business before we have to take care of business."

I nodded. After he'd darted out of the room, I realized, to my surprise, that *I* was hungry.

"We've got a few minutes," I said. "How about I Make something really quick? When the time comes, we might as well hurl ourselves into the unknown on a full stomach." I was already up, anyway.

Marta smiled down at me. "*Majera* specials?"

I shrugged. "Unless you're tired of them."

"They're quick and easy."

"That's what I figured," I said.

Brushing past her, I was conscious of her warmth and her current scent, spicy. It was comforting. I found myself giving her a one-armed hug on the way. She pressed her hand to my shoulder and made it a full hug, squeezing me tight before letting me go with a quiet, "Thank you."

I made my way dizzily to the wardroom.

The *Majera* specials were palm-sized pastries, filled with something that tasted like schnitzel but was really gluten protein. Marta had come up with them on our first trip, and they'd become a staple of our existence. We all had our customized favorites: Fareedh's were flavored with mint, Peter liked curry. Marta and I both liked sweet varieties. Sirena's specials tasted like nothing I'd ever had before, way spicier than I was used to. They were Pinky's favorite, too.

My eyes stung at the memory. Reflexively, I pulled out my *sayar*, calling up the holo of Pinky's room. He was still a cyan ball, unmoving. His life signs were still going, the weird organ that served as a heart beeping away a pulse at about half normal speed. It didn't look like he'd want food.

The specials were done in less than a minute, piping hot but without much aroma until opened. I'd forgotten to Make a plate under them, so I had to bat them gingerly onto a spare we'd made at breakfast before Jump-out. Peter came in from his cabin as I was leaving, and we did a little dance at the door getting back to the bridge.

Fareedh was waving at us as we entered. "He's there. Just got the message." He gestured to the display floating above my panel. I handed off the plate to him and stepped forward to read it.

"Made it. Tapping in. Wish L'éclair was here. Wait over."

"Who in the world is 'L'éclair'," Sirena asked, a crease between her arched eyebrows.

I knew that one. I took a pastry and sat down. "That's what Navy folks call their comms officer. It goes back centuries. L'éclair means..." I didn't know the Spanish word for lightning so I made the sound of thunder and drew a zigzag with my hand.

At the princess' impressed look, I smiled around a bite and mumbled, "I read a lot of space romance."

Fareedh bit into his special, made a face, and looked up at Peter. "I think I got yours. Trade?"

Peter frowned, chewing the bite from his own. "Yeah, I think you're right." He exchanged his nibbled-on pastry with Fareedh's, immediately taking another bite. He was clearly hungrier than he'd thought.

Another message: "*The system is open. Establishing a link via private channel. Over.*"

"Oho!" Fareedh called. Looking over his shoulder, I could see lines of text scrawling across his display. It was painfully slow. It took a full ten seconds to load.

"It's like transcribing semaphore," Marta noted.

"Maybe slower," Fareedh agreed. "There's not a lot of bandwidth on this channel. There's only so subtle I'll be able to be."

"What does that mean?" I asked.

"It means if I try to cut off life support or dim lights in local areas, they'll be able to respond faster than I can. Not that I know for sure where the bad folks are, except for the bridge, which will have back-ups anyway."

Sirena drifted closer to Fareedh. "Can you immobilize them or turn off their weapons?"

He mused a moment. Then, "I don't think so. Again, they'll re-act faster. Plus, that'll tip them off that someone's in the system and they'll start searching hardpoints. Hmm."

"Can't Iskender just work it from his end?" That seemed a lot easier to me.

Fareedh gave me an apologetic smile. "Iskender's a quartermas-ter. I'm the programmer in the family."

"Oh."

"Give a moment. Let me think a sec."

My left hand drifted to my panel and drummed a silent tattoo. I watched Fareedh work his lips right to left as he considered. Then his features smoothed and he leaned forward to tap away vigorously. Af-ter a few times trying to work directly with the display, with its slug-gish interface taking seconds to refresh, he cursed softly and opened up a new display, typing directly into that and copying it into the first. A minute went by. Two. Peter coughed, and we all looked up. He shook his head. He hadn't anything to say.

At last, Fareedh looked up from his display, turned to face us. "All right. I think I've got it."

"What's up?" I asked.

"I think I found us. *Majera*, I mean. On their scanner."

I coughed to clear my dry throat. "That's good news?"

"Yeah. There's no flags associated with it. We're a rock to them, and not on an intercept course. A harmless rock."

Peter scratched a burly shoulder. "That changes the second we move toward them, yeah?"

Fareedh waggled his eyebrows. "Not if we disable the flags associated with our contact."

"Won't they see us?" Sirena asked. "On their, how do you say, "scope"?"

"They might. But I doubt it. We're much closer than any other ships around. I'm betting they're mostly watching wide range scans, if that. They'll rely on the ship's *sayar* to report dangerous changes in state." He smiled up at Sirena. "And according to their ship's *sayar*, we aren't dangerous. We might as well not exist."

"How long will it take you to disable the flags?" I asked.

He went quiet in consideration again. "Normally, I'd say 15 minutes. I just have to hoax credentials and override the flag. But with this delay…" He snapped his fingers. "*This*, maybe Iskender can do."

His message went out on my display as well as his: "*Any nav or helm crew with you? Over.*"

The response was quick: "*A damage control specialist who says she's got helmsman certification. Over.*"

"*That works. Have her sign in. If the helm interface is an option, we're set. Over.*"

Marta spoke up nervously, "Won't that give them away?"

Fareedh shook his head. "Maybe, but I doubt they're monitoring the access of all of the crew. They'll only notice if she does something they don't like."

Out of the corner of my eye, I saw Sirena cross the fingers of her right hand.

"*She has access. Over.*"

Tap tap tap. "*Have her go to the medium-range scanner, select object T312, and disable all warnings. Over.*"

The chronometer ticked away seventeen seconds. The bridge fans cycled once, removing excess carbon dioxide from the air.

"Done. Over."

"Phew!" Fareedh gusted, leaning back and making an elaborate show of crossing his legs. He wore a smug smile. He tapped once more. *"What quarter should we approach at? Over."*

"Larboard lower. Minimum of ports and closer to us. Over," came the quick reply.

"That gets us *to* the *Faucon.* How do we get *in?*" I asked.

"Sure, expect me to think of everything," Fareedh said. His smile didn't fade.

"Well, think of something. You've got exactly as much time as it takes for us to get there minus five minutes," I said.

"Rodger dodg…" His voice caught on Pinky's signature expression. He coughed and said, instead, "Aye, aye."

The approach was tricky. I didn't want to use the main engines too close to the *Faucon* — the bright light would surely attract someone's or something's attention, especially when I had to turn around to decelerate, pointing fusion flame right at them. On the other hand, the antigrav unit still showed a worrisome yellow on the Tree. I was afraid to push it too hard. The only consolation was that fuel wasn't an issue, thanks to whatever the heck Drive innovation Peter had come up with.

Luckily, orbital mechanics were on our side. Both *Majera* and *Faucon* were in pretty circular paths around Hyvilma, and close to the same inclination. If either of us had had too much eccentricity or had been in different planes, the maneuver I was going to do would have been a lot harder. That we were so favorably aligned hadn't been a coincidence, I realized. The *Faucon* must have been waiting for ships near today's designated Jump-out zones. If we'd had our transponder on when we came into normal space, that'd have been the end of it.

I mouthed a voiceless prayer in thanks.

Comparatively easy or not, by the time *Faucon* was a slender speartip half-filling the Window, even at zero magnification, my tanktop was sticky with sweat. Twice, the thrusters had redlined, and I'd felt a queasy churn in my stomach as the internal gravity tried to do two things at once: maintain our movement and keep the cabin gees steady. I backed off in a hurry both times. The whole while, I expected a searing beam of light or the *pop* of decompression. All it would take was some vigilant observer to spot us and blow us out of space.

But, we made it, "parked" in orbit behind and to the left of the giant cruiser. Eight huge nozzles were round pits. If the *Faucon* decided it wanted to be somewhere else while we were here, chances were we'd get fried in an instant. My fingers itched.

"Tell 'em we're here," I half-squeaked.

The answer took longer than I'd expected, which made me all kinds of nervous. It didn't do any good to be this close if we couldn't get in.

Finally, *"Sorry for the wait. We moved from the hardpoint just in case. Scouted port hangar. No good. Guarded. There is a way in from here but you won't like it. Over."*

"There is so much otherwise to enjoy about the situation," Sirena observed, giving Peter a wink. That got a short laugh from him.

At Fareedh's expectant look, I just twirled my hand in a "go on" gesture. He conveyed it in text to his brother.

Peter said dolefully, "I think I know what he's gonna suggest." He was poring over a schematic of the *Faucon*, a close-up of the quarter currently facing us.

Iskender's answer came: *"We're about 50 meters from a chaff dispenser. We can jam open the door..."*

Er...

"You'll have to be quick. That'll give us away for sure..."

My lips slid back between my teeth.

"Coordinates X-103, Y-59, Z-25, datum: fusion chamber center. Let us know when you're there. Over."

I felt a scream gurgling somewhere deep inside me.

Peter seemed to deflate. "I knew it," he sighed, throwing his display over to the Window. The *Faucon* schematic expanded, zooming in on a circular indentation. A yellow glowing box popped up over it, with coordinates matching what Iskender had sent. A helpful scale appeared, too, indicating that the port was maybe two meters wide. We'd have to get to the hull of the cruiser, stand there with nothing but suit between us and vacuum, and then squeeze our way inside. Presumably while alarm bells went off throughout the *Faucon* and soldiers scrambled toward us with guns at the ready.

An insistent ping broke the silence. I jumped in my seat before I realized it was an internal comm. From Pinky!

"What are you doing awake?" I demanded.

Pinky's voice had a fuzzy quality to it, but otherwise sounded like him. "I got bored. I've been listening in the past stretch. We're boarding the *Faucon*?"

"Not we!" Marta exclaimed. "You're not going anywhere! You're sick."

"You haven't thought things through. I don't want to be on *Majera* once the mutineers notice us. They're liable to blow it up." A small 'eep' escaped my lips. "Sorry, Kitra," he added.

I *hadn't* thought things through. The moment we were inside, the *Faucon* was likely to do a close-range scan, see *Majera* parked next to her, and blast it out of an abundance of caution. My stomach roiled, and sweat flashed anew on my forehead.

"Pinky, we could go out and then you could take *Majera* away," I said hoarsely.

"I could, but then I'd be in the middle of nowhere in a ship I can't really drive. And if there's a doctor who can help me on the *Faucon*, they'll be that much further away." His voice went on with a whistling undertone. "I don't feel so good, Kitra."

Peter said incredulously, "And you want to join a boarding party?!"

"I want to get *better*," Pinky said.

"If we could get *Majera* away from the *Faucon*," Fareedh offered, "even just a bit, it might not be obviously linked with us. I could program a simple thruster fire to create some separation."

"Yeah," Peter said, "but how do we get from *Majera* to the cruiser without a link? I'm no space marine. I don't know the first thing about flying in no-gee, and we don't have any jet packs anyway."

He was right. The normal thing to do would be to anchor our two ships together with a cable with a magnetic tip and then clamber to the other side. If *Majera* was to be far enough away when we entered the *Faucon*, we'd have to be floating in space for a long time before we made our move, with no easy way to get from there to the cruiser.

"If we only had an air-car," I said bitterly. It had been on my list of priorities since I got our spaceship, but always financially out of reach, even with the Atlántidan princess backing us.

Sirena rotated her chair to face me, and a smile touched the corners of her lips. "Indeed…" she said, maneuvering gently, up and down. I blinked, then got it.

"You?"

"I must confide, I've always wanted to be a teamster."

Fareedh chuckled. "Is it vacuum-proof?" he asked.

"I should hope so," she said.

Peter broke in. "Let me get this straight," he said. "We'll leave the ship, send *Majera* away, and then you'll tow us to the *Faucon*? That's the most ridiculous plan I've ever heard in my life," he said.

Sirena turned to dispute him, but he was still talking. "…but, it's also the best one we've got. What the hell." He eyed me. "Think the ship's big enough for two heroes?"

The commed voice rasped. "Three! Don't forget me."

"Would you ever let me?"

"Not in this lifetime."

Marta gave Peter's shoulder a squeeze. "You're a hero already, love."

"Yes, yes," Sirena said with an imperious wave. "We're all overdue for holo stardom. The sooner we start, the sooner I can call my agent. Shall we?" She glided soundlessly toward the door, Peter and Marta stepping to one side, then following her through.

That left me and Fareedh. I watched him tap in firing instructions for the thrusters, to be triggered at his command. Turning to face me, he said, "That's that," and shrugged with a faint smile. He got up and offered his hand. I took it, and we went to join the others.

Chapter 10

We had to take turns leaving the ship. The airlock only fit two people at a time, and only one when the person was Sirena. She went first, then commed back to tell us she was ready. Fareedh went next, shrugging into his rainbow-patterned suit, and then suiting up Pinky in the vacuum-proof, flexible outfit he'd worn on the *Émilie*. Marta and Peter took turns checking each other's suits, tightening air tank seals, giving each other pats on the butt. I looked away from the monitor, down at the deck. When I looked back, the airlock had already cycled, the room empty and refilling with air.

Now it was just me. Captain is the last to leave the ship and all that. I hit the inner lock door button and put my helmet on before second thoughts could paralyze me. My hands trembled as they worked the final seals on my collar. They shook as I cycled the inner door. My whole body started to shiver as the outer door opened with a quickly fading *whoosh*, and there was nothing between me and the stars.

Allez-oop.

I collided with Peter and rebounded, flailing. He caught me with a strong hand and hooked a line to my belt. I made the mistake of looking down.

A yawning abyss of stars spread beneath me. I was going to *fall*! I tried to spin around, make my way back to the ship. But all I managed to do was writhe awkwardly on the line.

"Are you okay, Kitra?" Marta's voice.

No. I'm scared to death, suspended over an abyss a million light years deep.

"I'm fine," I croaked. I became aware of a warm feeling around my waist and crotch. Oh Lord. I'd peed my pants. My hands went unconsciously to my hips, then fluttered back up. At least the suit was made for this. The warmth faded as the moisture was absorbed and reclaimed.

Peter steadied me by the shoulders, then pressed his helmet to mine. I heard him say in the open air rather than over comms, "Me, too," with a rueful laugh. He pointed at his crotch. "Mighty heroes."

I reached out for his hand and gripped it. He winced audibly, and I loosened my hold a touch. "I'm fine," I reassured again over the comms. "I've never not had a floor or ground before. I'll be alright." My pounding heart called me a liar, but I didn't need to compound everyone else's worry.

We were a thick clump of people, slowly adrift with respect to each other, but all within a meter of a common center. Behind us, *Majera* was a featureless, white, stubby-winged bird, the lock door having closed up by itself. Above, from our perspective, lay the long bulk of the *Faucon*. Besides that, it was all stars, in every direction. It's dizzying enough to be confronted with thousands of twinkling suns when you're on your back, stargazing far from town. It's another to view a starfield from the comfort of a pressurized, gravitized bridge.

Being *in* the stars, millions of searing pinpoints…I didn't know if I could ever get used to this. Some intrepid explorer I was.

"Shall I send *Majera* on her way?" Fareedh asked. A muscle left of my navel cramped at the thought of sending our ship away. It wasn't too late to turn back…

"Do it," I managed.

Slowly at first, soundlessly all the while, *Majera* receded into the starfield. I watched it until it was no brighter than any of the other points of light. I blinked, and I lost it. Gone.

Just us, in a clump, alone in space.

"Did you ever play 'Crack the Whip'?" That was Sirena.

Fareedh answered. "I'm afraid I don't know that one."

"I am about to go. I'll try to keep as straight a course as I can, but, Kitra, you will want to hold the line firmly."

No sooner had she said that, than my fingers were clutching the tether. Sirena started to drift toward the cruiser. Her chair was hidden inside a fuzzy ellipsoid — the same shield she'd used when she'd faced off the squatters on Purité. I suppose if it was proof against beamers, it made sense it would also be vacuum-tight. We began to separate along the line like a chain of pearls. Peter jerked away from me with a *woof*, and then suddenly I was being yanked at the waist, legs sailing behind me. It would have been worse if I hadn't been holding on to the line.

The loudest noise was the sound of my breathing, heavy and hollow in the helmet. But for a moment, I thought I heard the others, too, a chorus of whispering breaths in high and low registers. No one spoke as the *Faucon* grew from a wand in the sky to a wall blotting out half the starscape. That was just as well. Even turned down to the lowest power setting, our comms could be picked up this close to the cruiser.

About halfway there, the dim egg that was Sirena in her chair drifted sideways a couple of meters, then flew back along the line, like a snake curling back on itself. As she passed Pinky, he joined her new course, followed by the others and finally me, spinning me around with a jolt. Now she was thrusting the other way, decelerating. I looked over my shoulder at the looming cruiser. I wasn't holding up the rear anymore—I was going to make first contact! My heart moved up to somewhere just under my throat.

I slid the belt-loop around behind me so at least I'd be facing *Faucon* when we made contact. We were close enough that I could see the contours in the gray hull, dimly lit by lights far to the aft and fore of the ship. I couldn't be sure what any of the anonymous bumps, bulges, and indentations were, much less which one was the chaff port.

The last few meters seemed to take an eternity. I had to hand it to Sirena; either she was an instinctive space traveler, or her chair had a very sophisticated *sayar* on board, because I made touchdown on the *Faucon* as lightly as a feather-seed's landing. I quickly magnetized my boots so I wouldn't bounce off. In short order, the rest had landed next to me. I anxiously looked at Pinky, back to being a round ball, who rebounded upon hitting the hull and did nothing about it. Marta and Fareedh wrestled him against the *Faucon*, holding him steady with their lines. I wanted to call out to him, but of course, I couldn't.

The lanky silhouette that was Fareedh pointed to his *sayar* and at the hull of the ship, trudging one careful step at a time toward one of the bulges. We had no choice but to follow him; I assumed he was heading to the coordinates his brother had sent him. I hesitated when it was my turn to lift a foot from the hull, but the tug at my belt was irresistible, and off I went, half walking, half drifting. At the protrusion, no more than a meter up from the hull, he stopped and gave us a thumbs up. Then he waved his arms wildly at the bump to make his point. This was it.

I made my way up next to him, Peter close behind me since he was still tethered to my back. Fareedh clicked his helmet against mine. "I'll signal my brother now," he called out. I nodded back, and he did something with his *sayar*.

Nothing happened. For a while.

Sweat was starting to prickle me at my joints, despite the wicking actions of the suit. I looked from side to side, half-expecting a squad of marines to pop up onto the hull, rifles at the ready. Then I made the mistake of looking "up", and the naked stars gave me vertigo again.

A loud "clack" set my heart pounding again. But it was just Fareedh locking helmets to talk again. He pointed at the deck's bulge. It wasn't a slate hill anymore, but a crater with an inky, featureless mouth. It was open!

Fareedh wore an exultant grin. I smiled weakly back. Maybe it made more sense for him to go first. But I was the one at the end of the line. At the other end was Sirena, and I had no idea what Iskender's group would make of her chair if it came soaring in before us. I stepped to the lip of the crater and knelt to grab hold of the edge. I demagnetized my boots, and with a tug, sailed inside.

…and almost immediately thudded against a wall, bouncing backward. I instinctively threw my hands wide to catch the rim of the chaff port so I wouldn't fly back out into space. I felt steadying hands on my back; Peter's probably. One more try, and this time, I flicked on the suit lamps. The chamber was smaller than I'd thought, barely enough room for me to curl up inside. Getting Sirena through was going to prove a challenge. Well, one thing at a time.

There was no obvious way to open the portal into the ship, nor did I have any clue what was on the other side. I floated there, bemused for a moment. At last, I shrugged and scratched at the smooth hatch, like a cat. Almost immediately, it irised open. I braced myself for a gust of air, but none came. Instead, I was looking at a filmy wall, translucent and a little slimy-looking. An emergency seal, I realized. They'd made a make-shift airlock. Smart. It might take longer for alarm bells to go off this way, without an abrupt decompression.

I gave Peter a thumbs up, then unhooked my line. With a quick shove, I went into the yielding material. It was like swimming through whipped cream, only the slightest resistance, and the gel kept a tight seal around me the whole way, losing no air.

The moment I was through, I fell to the deck inside with a thud. There was gravity here. Racked around me were neatly stowed cylinders about a meter long. Those would be the chaff dispensers, filled with millions of shards designed to confuse enemy sensors. The containers only took my attention for a moment, though. Light streamed in through an open hatch about two meters opposite the film-covered port. Silhouetted against it was a figure in naval uniform. They were tapping something into their *sayar*. Then they surged forward, reaching out to help me to my feet.

"You're Kitra, right?" His muffled voice sounded like a tenor version of Fareedh's.

I doffed my helmet. "Iskender, yeah?"

He nodded. "Let's clear the way. I told them to come on through. We've only got a minute." Fareedh's brother hustled me out into the corridor, where I counted three others. One, like Iskender, wore the black and silver formal tunic of a ship's officer, but with only a single stripe on his sleeve. The other two, both women, were in gray coveralls. Whether that meant they were crew or simply got caught out of uniform, I couldn't tell.

The older of the two "crew" was a striking woman, her short hair shot through with gray. "I'm glad you're here. And happy to see you brought some muscle with you." She jerked a thumb at Peter, edging his bulk into the passageway.

"That's me," he said. "Mr. Muscles."

"That's not the one to look out for," I said, a little giddy with adrenalin. Marta came through, looking every bit the space marine in her green jumpsuit, a beamer at both hips. She struck a pose and grinned like a feral cat. There was a pause, presumably while Fareedh was giving Pinky a hand. I had a moment to study Iskender. It was hard to believe he and Fareedh came from the same family, let alone were siblings. Fareedh had skin as dark as mine, and jet-black hair. Iskender was fair and blond. Where Fareedh moved with relaxed ease, Iskender was all nervous tension.

There was no mistaking their connection once Fareedh got in the ship, however. The two brothers wrapped each other in a fierce hug, Fareedh doffing his helmet and wiping away tears. I was surprised to see Pinky straggle in on his own power and three stumpy legs, trotting up to the side-by-side brothers. He even grew a little arm and saluted.

"The party can start. I'm here," he said.

The sound of padded footsteps rushing down the hall drew our attention. Marta unclipped a beamer and held it steady. Iskender touched her shoulder, in negation. A young, brown-haired ensign skidded into view.

"We've got to hurry. They've started a patrol in this section." Their eyes widened. "Hey! You got L'éclair!"

I looked up at Iskender, who was shaking his head. "No, he's up on Deck Six."

The officer looked disappointed, then fearful. "Well, let's get going."

Iskender turned to me. "You've got one left, right?"

Peter answered, "Yeah, but…" He looked dubiously at the portal. "There's no way she'll fit through there with her field on."

My mind raced. If she couldn't get in, the only other option was going back. Could she make her way back to the ship? No way. *Majera* was dozens of kilometers away by now, maybe hundreds.

"She's got to come in. She's not wearing a suit?" I asked.

"No," Pinky wheezed. "The princess hates wearing them, like me."

Fareedh added, "Sirena's not going anywhere without her chair, anyway."

"Folks, we have to hurry," the young officer said, more agitated.

My hands fluttered. "How do we even get a message to her? You and Iskender are the only ones who can talk without giving us away," I said to Fareedh.

Marta reached for her helmet. "I can go out and tell her…" She paused halfway to the hatch. "Except I can't knock my helmet against anything."

"Maybe tug on the line," Peter said excitedly. He looked down, saw the tether hanging loosely. "No, I had to cut loose to get inside."

"Now, folks!" the officer hissed.

A crash followed by a coughing fit arose from beyond the hatch. I rushed in and gaped in horrified surprise. Sirena's chair was tipped sideways just in front of the glistening makeshift airlock, the princess half spilled out on the deck of the chaff chamber. Her bronze skin was pale and dry-looking. She must have turned off her shield to squeeze her chair through the gelled port. The chair hadn't been able to adjust to the sudden gravity change, and she'd flown out of her seat. The smooth leglessness beyond her waist that tapered to powerful fins was hooked on the rim of the chair. She was like a stranded fish. I rushed up to her.

"Are you all right?" I babbled.

Between coughing gulps of air, she managed a weak nod and a smile.

"We've got to hurry, Sirena," I urged. "The mutineers are coming."

"Help me back in," she gasped. I had no idea how to work the chair. Instead, I just pressed against her shoulders, supporting her as she pushed with thin arms and dainty, webbed hands. Worming side to side, she slid back into place, the chair immediately pivoting upright with respect to the deck. I backed into the corridor to give her room to leave. Her chair just made it through the narrow opening.

"Sorry I'm late," she sang in low tones. "Shall we go?"

Chapter 11

Iskender's hidey hole turned out to be some kind of storage hold. A half dozen racks with magnetic or grav grips bulged with spare parts. Hull sheeting, electrical components, junctions, mounts, and more gleamed dimly in the low light. There were no complex pieces of equipment, and definitely no weapons. It must have been a damage control depot.

It was also very cramped, the thirteen of us occupying virtually all the open space, even with our helmets collapsed and hooked to our backs. Sirena's chair hovered at the entrance; it wouldn't fit between the racks. There was a quick round of introductions, but the only names that stuck belonged to the older woman in coveralls, who was called Aylin, and the young woman who'd been the other guard, unseen when we came out of the portal. She had short curly hair, and her name was Deniz. She wore the crossed screwdriver and spanner insignia of a technician on her black, enlisted tunic.

"What's the plan, Lieutenant Konak?" Sirena asked briskly.

Iskender looked nonplussed a moment, as if the question took him by surprise.

"Well, I can't imagine the whole ship has gone mutinous," he said. "They've got the bridge for sure, and a bunch of armed people on patrol." He thought for a moment. "A lot of the crew who weren't in on it were put into the enlisted barracks. They must be guarded. If we could free them, we might have the numbers we need."

The flaw in his plan was obvious. I'd read enough space dramas. "More people would help," I spoke up, "but so long as they've got the bridge and maybe other nerve centers, they can close off passageways, shut off air, set a self-destruct sequence. We've got to hit them everywhere at once."

"With a dozen against who knows how many?" Peter objected.

"We'll have the advantage of surprise," Deniz countered.

A muffled voice came from behind me. Pinky, who I'd thought had slipped into unconsciousness again, was stirring. "Perhaps if we had a map," he said, "we could better visualize the situation." He was armless, standing on a stumpy tripod of legs, an eyespotted bluish lump sticking out from his suit.

To Iskender's credit, he didn't seem alarmed by the alien. I guessed Navy folks were used to more unusual things than most. Fareedh's brother pulled out his *sayar* to project a holo in front of him, a schematic of the *Faucon*, I quickly realized.

"We're here," he said, pointing to a spot near the aft of the ship. "The enlisted quarters are on the lower decks, right here." Iskender indicated a spot about a third of the way up the ship, just forward of what looked like the power plant. "The bridge is amidships on Deck Two. Ordnance isn't centralized. There are batteries here, here, and here." The turrets stayed lit as he touched them, a ring of beam and missile emplacements girdling the ship. "There's sensor command information center, fore of the bridge. And then there's auxiliary control, here." That was a small room three decks down and just aft of the bridge.

"That's too many targets," said the officer who had spotted the search party earlier. They were an ensign, I realized, and quite young.

"We'll have to prioritize." That was Fareedh.

"What have you got in mind, bro?"

Fareedh considered. "If we could shut the plant down, that'd silence the turrets and prevent a self-destruct."

His brother shook his head. "The engineers are in on it, at least enough of them. I don't think we can get in there."

"Maybe not physically," Fareedh said meaningfully.

"You mean hack the software?"

"Maybe, or have sufficient access to just key in the command."

Iskender considered. "You'd need a better hard access point than the one I was using. Something with O4 authority or higher."

"That's going to be the bridge, sensor CiC, or auxiliary control,"

Aylin offered.

"What's the easiest target?" Fareedh asked.

"Definitely the auxcon. Easier than the other two, anyway," his brother said.

"So, what?" Peter asked. "We rush in, turn out the lights, and then free the prisoners?"

"Something like that, I guess," Iskender said. "We'd need to split up."

It hit me then just what we were talking about. A bare dozen of us, half of us civilians, the other half supply clerks and techs, were talking about taking on a band of armed killers. Worse still, *we'd* have to be killers, or at least prepared to be. I wasn't Admiral Okafor or Captain Hornblower. I certainly wasn't James Bond or The Mist. I felt myself starting to tremble, and my vision blurred. The *Faucon* crew were black smudges, their talk meaningless echoes.

Something touched my hand, and I jerked back, as if shocked. Marta looked down at me, surprise and worry touching her green eyes.

"Kitra, I said, 'Are you alright?'"

I was anything but alright. I opened my mouth to speak, but my throat was a desert.

Her hand gripped mine, her eyes softening. "I *know*. But we'll make it. We have to." She looked behind me, and I followed her gaze. To Pinky, now a legless hemisphere, just his "head" poking out of his suit. I licked my lips, staring at my oldest friend, and felt the fear retreat, just a little bit, pushed aside by the need to get him help.

I looked back at Marta, who gave me a little nod. I took a bracing breath, then cocked my head. Something had occurred to me. "Are *you* okay?" I asked.

She blinked. "I…sure. What do you mean?" she whispered back.

"You're so *va-t'en guerre*, so pumped up." I looked at the deck. "I know how you feel about the Empire. These people we're going to face, they're fighting the Empire."

Marta's expression went pensive. "It's something I'm trying not to think too hard about. Right now, we hardly know anything about what's going on. One recorded message isn't enough to go on."

She smiled softly and tilted up my chin with the fingers of her free hand. "Anyway, right now politics can hang. Nothing matters more than family." The pressure on my hand became a hard squeeze, and Marta's eyes were shining. Mine stung too, I realized.

I looked at her for what seemed a good long time. She'd never looked lovelier, determination setting her soft features. My heart started to thud again, but for an entirely different cause.

I felt myself take a step toward her, eyes half shut, lips upturned. Panic set in, and instead I threw my arms around her in an awkward hug. If Marta noticed how weird the whole thing had been, she didn't give anything away. She just wrapped her arms around me and squeezed.

It came to me that the conversation the others were having had faltered. I looked at them, saw them looking at me.

I coughed. "What?"

"You two okay?"

"Yes," I answered. "Just discussing. Do we have a plan?" I realized I still had one arm draped around Marta's waist, mirroring hers around mine. I moved a step to my left, and put my hands on my hips.

"Yeah," Iskender said. "Same plan as before. Half of us will hit the auxiliary control. The rest will free the prisoners. We were just figuring out who should go with whom."

"I want us to stick together," I said.

"What, all of us?" Iskender asked.

"No, I mean the *Majera* crew."

Peter gestured, elbow in one of his huge hands, "We're going to want at least one of them as a guide."

"That's fine," I said, looking back at Iskender. "So seven on our team, six on yours."

"Seven? You're taking your…your friend with you? He's so sick he can't even walk."

"Pinky comes with us," I said firmly.

"We've only got five guns between us," Fareedh observed. "Marta's beamers, two stunners, and a gummer. Can we get more?"

His brother shrugged. "Maybe. The armories are going to be guarded, and the first thing they did was disarm the officers."

"We can improvise," Marta said with a grin, patting her bag.

"I've got some knock-out hypos. And I don't need both of these." She pulled out one of her beamers and looked as if she was about to offer it to me, then instead handed it to Fareedh. I exhaled in relief. I didn't want a lethal weapon in my hands.

"What kind of arms will they have, Lieutenant?" Sirena asked.

"Same as us, I guess. Without the beamers. They're not standard issue. Too much risk of hurting the ship."

"That is good. Less need for my services if their weapons cannot kill."

"God willing." He used the Turkish phrase, *inşallah*.

Fareedh echoed the phrase, adding, "It makes sense for you and me to split up. You've got the magic *sayar*, and we'll need to coordinate our moves."

"Yeah." He looked at his crewmates. "Any volunteers to take on the bridge?"

Aylin stepped forward. "Sounds like fun," she said.

I nodded to her gratefully. "There's really no time to lose, then. Our team will comm you when we get to the aux con. When we head for the bridge, I guess that's when you go for the barracks."

A crackling sound punctuated my words, causing me to jump in my boots. It was Peter, the knuckles of a curled fist in the other hand. He looked up at me sheepishly.

"Ready when you are," he said.

Chapter 12

I padded down the corridor, one of Marta's hypos clutched in my fingers, understanding just how a stonebug feels stuck out in a clearing under a circling yarasa bird. We walked two abreast, Pinky on my left. Marta's curls bounced in front of me. Behind every door we passed, I imagined a half-troop of guards, ready to burst out at us. My senses stabbed at me–the faint rubbery scent in the air, the occasional flicker of the ceiling panels, and especially our footsteps, which sounded painfully loud.

"We're going to get picked up on someone's screen," Peter whispered behind me.

"Could be," Fareedh murmured back. "Maybe I should have worn something less conspicuous."

"Do you have such a thing?" Pinky wheezed.

"Guys, could you shut up?" I hissed.

Our shuffling steps became the loudest sounds again. Aylin left Marta's side to peer around the corner, then gave us a curt wave. We turned right to head single-file through a narrow passage designed for quick maintenance access rather than regular crew travel. It was less kept up, and a few faint stains showed where coolants and lubricants had been spilled. I took a quick look behind me, noting with relief that Sirena's chair, bringing up the rear, was able to squeeze into the narrow hall. The hum of machinery and fans covered our sounds, which was nice.

A left took us into a wider corridor, a maintenance section, if the plates on the doors were any indication. Shops, parts, stores. This end of the ship where we'd come aboard had to be where damage control teams worked their magic to replace broken equipment. Peter would be right at home.

I managed not to crash into Marta's back. She'd stopped suddenly, Aylin's arm slashing right across her chest. The spacer had her head cocked, listening. Then she hissed, "Scatter!"

I grabbed Pinky's paw and looked frantically for an exit. There was a door to my right. I slammed my palm against the black pad just right of its jamb. Nothing. Locked! By the time I turned around, the passage was cleared, and other doors, ones more obliging than mine had been, were closing. A low mechanical whine filled the corridor, coming from just around the next corner. There was nowhere to hide; if we darted for another door now, we'd surely be seen. I couldn't run and leave Pinky behind, either. The sound grew louder. I swallowed. This was it, then. I gripped the hypo like an amulet and mouthed a prayer.

A black oval robot, a meter wide and half as tall, trundled into the passage on treads. My breath caught. It rode straight toward me at a slow walking pace. If it was a security mech, we were as good as dead.

The mech came straight toward us, approaching to within a few paces. I caught a sharp whiff of something acrid, and when we backed against the walls of the corridor, it continued past as if we weren't there at all, leaving the deck glistening with a sheen of moisture.

A cleaning robot!

My legs felt like noodles. I sagged against the wall, my joints prickling. Pinky slid an eyespot over to face me.

"Someone rolled well for their random encounter," he said, the blue skin of his head tingeing more lavender for a moment.

"If only this was a game of *Starsagas*," I panted.

I went to the door I'd seen Fareedh duck into and rapped, two longs and a short, the code we'd agreed on. The door slid open, and Fareedh stood there, hands on hips. He'd managed to find a grease-stained jacket while he was in the room, which he'd put over the riot of colors that was his suit. His legs were still clad in skin-tight rainbows, though.

With Fareedh's help, we soon got the rest of the team back into the corridor.

"Couldn't we, I dunno, go through an air vent or something?"

Marta was asking Aylin.

"You've watched too many holodramas. They're not a meter wide on this ship or any other. Anyway, it's not like your friend would fit." The crewperson gestured at Sirena.

"Perhaps we might," Sirena said in low, musical tones, "devise a better solution than calling out 'scatter' for next time?" I nodded in agreement

"This isn't exactly my specialty," Aylin said with a touch of testiness. "I'm in records." She considered a moment. "Tell you what. As we go through each corridor, I'll point to the path we should go to hide. But it's just going to be an educated guess."

We started off again, though now I had even less confidence in our expedition. At the next intersection, Aylin stopped, like a cat sniffing the air. She pointed toward a stairwell just ahead. I frowned. Was that our hiding spot? Then she actually headed into it, and I realized she wanted us to follow her. So much for our "system".

Up we went, our steps ringing hollowly on the metal stairs, with Sirena's chair a low whirr underlying the sound.

"If we'd kept forward," Aylin explained over her shoulder, "we'd have run into the larboard armory."

We left the stairwell two levels up. In contrast to the grimy functionality of the damage control deck, this corridor could have been located in any office or public building, except for the uncarpeted, hullmetal floor. My throat tightened with unease. The gray paint, the white linteled doors, all of it gave me an inexplicable feeling of impending doom. Then I realized what it looked like: Education deck on *L'émissaire*, which I'd last seen on my way to an escape pod. The fingers of my right hand flicked against each other as we walked. *That was a decade ago*, I told myself. The *Faucon* was not likely to explode in some freak accident. There was plenty else to worry about.

Aylin waved at the closed door marked "Purser." Since we walked on past it, I assumed she was marking our escape route. My guess was right as she marked another door two turns later. We were making good progress. I couldn't afford the time to steal a glance at my *sayar*, but we had to be at least a quarter of the way there already.

Just to my left, something clicked and rattled. I spun to see a door marked "WC-19" slide open. A young spacer in a black enlisted tunic stepped out, adjusting his trousers. He looked up, eyes widening, hands reaching for his holstered gun. His mouth opened as if to scream.

He never got the chance. Pinky pounced, not so much wrestling as engulfing him. One spacesuited pseudopod went straight into the man's mouth, strangling any sound, while another went around him, continuing until it met the core of Pinky's body, and merged.

"Knock him out!" Pinky rasped.

I lurched forward, but Fareedh had beaten me to it, ramming a sedative into what he could see of the man's neck. He sagged in Pinky's grip, and Pinky let him go, slowly returning to his more-or-less human configuration.

"He might have been a good guy," Peter said.

"He wasn't under guard," Aylin noted. "And anyway, I know him." She tsked with distaste. "I'm not surprised." She ran a hand through her short-cropped hair. "Well, that tears it. We've got a hard time limit now—the time it takes for someone to follow up on why he's not calling in."

Fareedh and Peter got the spacer back into the bathroom and locked the door from the inside before closing it. Fareedh offered Marta her beamer back; he had the spacer's side-arm in his other hand, a small black pistol that looked like a stunner. Marta took the beamer and stuck it back on her hip.

"Maybe we'll get lucky," Fareedh said with a weak smile. "Some people take a long time in the head. It's plausible, right?"

"Yeah, he's reading a really good book," I said, reaching for Pinky's mitt-like hand. I went to take a step, but Pinky didn't budge. I turned. He looked like he'd half melted into the floor, and he was an ugly shade of azure.

"We…may…have another…time constraint," he managed. "I don't feel…so…"

His fingers melded into a fin, which retreated into his body. He was a half-deflated balloon.

My hands fluttered. "Where's the sick bay on this ship?" I squeaked.

"But," Aylin protested, "what about the plan?"

"Pinky's not going to make it. He needs help right now," I hissed.

Aylin eyed Pinky. "Yeah. I guess you're right. Sickbay…The main one's amidships, fore of auxiliary control. Probably locked down," Aylin said.

"There must be others!" Marta said.

"Yeah," she said, nodding. "Yeah. There's stations larboard and starboard closer to us." She dug out her *sayar* and called up a schematic of the *Faucon*. "This one's probably doable," she said, pointing to the larboard one. "It's only active during battle stations." The spacer made a wry face. "Conventional battle stations, that is. You think we can do something for your friend there?"

Sirena spoke up, "We must try. In any event, it is another place to hide along the way."

Pinky wouldn't move. He looked dead. I wasn't even sure how to tell if he wasn't.

"I'm getting him out of the suit," I snapped. "He'll breathe better."

For a mad moment, I considered just ripping it from the hem of the ring that had been around Pinky's neck and was now just a circle on the alien's round form. But he might need it again, and I had no idea where we would get another one.

While I fumbled with it, Peter started to pace nervously. We were right out in the open. We could be caught any minute. My hands shook as I worked, and a growl of frustration rose in my throat.

Aha! At a pinch of pressure, the suit parted naturally, sliding off like gauze. I rolled Pinky out of his suit and pulled off the glove from mine. I licked my palm and pressed it to his skin. His body was warm, but every second or so, my hand cooled as he exhaled. I blew out a breath. Pinky was still with us.

I folded the tissue-paper of his suit, stuffed it in a pocket, and put my glove back on. Then I tried again to get Pinky to stand. No good. He was a fifty kilo bean bag, and just as responsive.

"We've got to carry him," I said. My first glance was to Sirena, but her chair didn't look big enough for the job. "We could do it with two people?" I added doubtfully. Marta knelt down next to me, and we tried to get a good grip on him, but he was an awkward bundle. We got him a meter off the floor and managed a couple of steps, Marta marching backwards. My hands trembled, threatening to slip.

"It's not going to work," I hissed.

Peter stage-whispered, "Hold him up a second more." Then, somehow, he had slid between us, bent nearly double under Pinky with his burly arms stretched backwards. "Okay, lower him onto me," he said.

I strained to keep from just dropping my friend, though my fingers were white with the effort. Peter took him in a boulder carry, straightening his legs despite the weight.

"Let's get going," he grunted.

"Right." Aylin nodded. "Ah…let's turn left up ahead. I have an idea."

We followed her, through what felt like a big detour from our destination. A dizzying mishmash of corridors and turns that made no sense. Between the confusing path and focusing on Aylin's pointing out hiding spots, I became thoroughly lost. Finally, we were in a corridor that was sharply distinct from the others. The wall on the right was the usual set of doors and occasional passages, but the left-hand wall was featureless and somehow tougher looking. As we paused for breath, I looked the question at Aylin.

"That's the hull of the ship," the spacer explained. "I figure there will be less traffic on the outer edges. This hall ends at the larboard wardroom. Through that, another hall, and then we're at the medbay."

"You don't think there will be people in the wardroom?" Marta asked nervously.

"It's for petty officers, and they're all locked up, on the bridge, or at duty stations, so far as we could tell."

I stole a glance at Peter. Except for a little flush to his face, he showed no sign of strain, matching our pace as we hastened down the hall. Aylin jogged ahead of us, keeping her steps as light as she could, to peer around the corner. Flashing a quick smile, she nodded and waved us off the accessway into a wider hall that ran perpendicular.

The second door to the left was marked "Chiefs' Mess". With a cautionary wave to stay back, Aylin nonchalantly threw the door open and walked in as if she belonged there. The rest of us stood exposed in the corridor for a sweat-prickling few seconds measured in minutes. Then she was back, ushering us in.

"Nobody here," she whispered.

The room was a bit bigger than the wardroom on the *Majera*. Dark wood paneling, or plastic made to look like it, wainscotted the lower halves of the walls behind a bunch of low-slung couches and empty tables. There was a commissary along the right wall with what looked like both manual and automatic fixtures. Across another wall, plaques, trophies, and wall sprawls dominated. Above all, there was a sense of *age*, of dirt and hookah smoke , and years of butts in seats making the cloth threadbare shiny.

I took this all in with a hasty look as we trotted across the anti-static rug done in checkerboard tile. On any other day, I'd have wanted to explore every cranny of the cozy-looking room. At this moment, my only concern was getting to the other side without someone coming in and spotting us. A loud clatter came from behind, causing both me and Marta to start. Whirling around, we saw it was just Peter, who had bumped a chair. He was stooped a bit lower under Pinky's weight now.

"I'm fine," he grunted. "Keep moving, please."

We went through the door at the far end of the wardroom, between a trophy case and an overstuffed chair. Aylin was already halfway up the hall. On the left, there was a door labeled "gym" and on the right...

"This is it," Aylin said, tapping the pad to open the door marked "Sick Bay, Compartment 13". It didn't budge. She palmed it again. Nothing.

"Is it locked?" Marta whispered.

"Yeah. Shit." The spacer rubbed her chin, considering it. "We could force it, but that'd trigger an alarm."

I turned to Fareedh. "Can you work your magic? Tell the ship's *sayar* to unlock it?"

He blinked, nonplussed a moment, then clicked his tongue in a negative. "I don't have access from here, and even then, it'd be a different subsection from the one I was playing with earlier. It'd take too long."

"Hold on," Peter said with a labored groan. He squatted, gently rolling Pinky off his back. Straightening out caused a chorus of cracks to come from his knees and hips. "Infinity, that guy is heavy," he said, but there was no heat to the words. "Alright. Let me look at it."

He gave the door a tentative tap, then pressed his palms against the portal and pushed towards the jamb they would slide into. There was a soft click.

"I said, don't force it," Aylin hissed.

"I'm not. But if this is a Navy ship, I'm willing to bet it's a simple magnetic lock. And installed by the lowest bidder." He pulled out something from his hip bag and extended it to a quarter-meter or so in length. Pressing his ear to the door, he looked like nothing so much as one of those old-time safecrackers from the last millennium. He ran his tool over the panel, twirled it a few times. There was another click. Now Peter lifted the tool like a baton, as if conducting an invisible orchestra. I heard a clunk, and the door slid open a crack.

Peter grunted and slid it the rest of the way. "Hopefully, that doesn't set anything off. It shouldn't. As far as the ship's *sayar* is concerned, the door is still closed."

"Depends on the system," Fareedh countered quietly.

"Trust me on this one," he said, crouching and nodding to Pinky's spherical form. "One more time?"

We hefted Pinky back onto Peter, who trudged into sick bay and poured him gently onto a bed. Pinky didn't respond, but he did sort of collapse a little. Yellow-outlined displays popped up over him, filled with medical words and graphs. He was vividly blue, now. My vision blurred, and I looked away, blinking back tears.

Sirena floated past me, tapping at the displays. After a moment, she gave a surprised, "A-ha!"

"What is it?" Marta asked.

"The ship's *sayar* is quite comprehensive. It called up baseline readings for Pinky's people almost immediately, without me querying it to do so."

"You mean it recognized what he was?" Fareedh asked.

"Yes. That should be helpful. Perhaps I can get a better diagnosis."

I looked up, hopeful, watching the Atlántidan doctor consult readings and tap through pages of text. She turned, her eyes scanning over the walls.

"I'm looking for the Med-Maker. Ah, there it is." Sirena explained as she flew to it, "Pinky's lost a lot of fluid, and he requires a specific hydrostatic balance. Plus nutrients. I must say, the information in the ship's *sayar* is most helpful." As she programmed the gray machine to produce what she needed, she said, "Marta, darling, can you set up the intravenous?"

"Of course, doctor," Marta replied. There was a portable device, something like a metal tree, on wheels rather than gravs, that she rolled over to the bed. "Loading bay is clean and empty."

"Good. Just give me a moment to brew this up."

I stole a glance at Pinky. He'd collapsed further. Normally, a ball was his natural resting shape. He looked like a ruined soufflé.

"We've got to hurry," I blurted.

"I've got it," Sirena said, floating back to his bedside. She handed a sloshing clear container to Marta, who installed it deftly.

"Where do we insert the IV?" Marta asked, perplexed. "It's not like he's got veins."

Sirena frowned, considering. "We don't." She tugged the injector tip off one of the flexible branches of the IV unit and extended the tube until its little mouth pressed directly against Pinky's skin. "Let's see if nature will do the work."

Seconds passed. Nothing happened.

"Patience," Sirena urged.

The IV machine gurgled softly. At the same time, Pinky shivered, once, and fluid coursed slowly through the clear tube. I closed my eyes and unballed my fists. My palms hurt where the nails had dug in.

"It's like watching a balloon inflate," I heard Peter say.

Pinky did look better when I opened my eyes, creases filling in, the dark blue fading. Now he was a giant lavender egg yolk.

"He was severely dehydrated," Sirena noted.

"I gave him water before we left," I said, hurt.

She put a hand on my wrist. "It's not your fault. He has a delicate balance to maintain. You couldn't have known what he needed. *I* didn't."

"Kitra," Pinky wheezed.

I pressed my cheek to his side. "I'm here," I choked out.

"Where..." was all he could manage.

"In sick bay. You're safe. Sirena's taking care of you."

He trembled slightly, pressing tears into my face. "Drifting," he said. "Here and not here." Strength grew in his voice, "You're all wet."

"That's *your* fault," I said, half laughing, half sobbing.

"Din't mean to drag you through sprinklers," he went on, his voice now sing-song, childlike. "They were so pretty. Like little rainbows. Never saw anything like it before." He giggled. "Prof Golan is going to be mad."

I pulled back and eyed my friend worriedly. Golan had been our third-grade teacher, and he *had* been mad. 13 years ago.

Twin eyespots drifted over his body, disconnected and aimless.

"Where is everybody?" he cried plaintively. "I can't see you."

"Everything's okay, buddy," Peter said, putting a broad hand on his flank. "We're all here."

That seemed to relax him. Then he flushed, alternating pink and a faded orange. "We are here…yes." His voice lost all tone, fading to a halting hiss. "All of us. Here…room place…this. Time place…this. Smell…smell like…" He spewed a scent like sour cumin and whispered a jumbled sound that made no sense. Something like *frelj*. It might have been the same word he'd used when telling us about his earliest memory. Pinky was almost fully round again, but now completely still.

"Pinky?" I called. No response. I looked up quickly at Sirena.

"I think he's unconscious," she said, frowning intently as his vital signs waved along. "He has stabilized."

"You mean he'll be alright?" Fareedh asked.

She shook her head. "He is in hydrostatic balance, but artificial sera can only get him so far. He will need some kind of transfusion."

"But Pinky's family's dozens of light years from here!" I exclaimed. Even if we made it through all this, could he survive a trip all the way back to Vatan?

I became aware of the sound of the sick bay door closing and looked up. Aylin was pacing quickly back to us. I hadn't realized she'd gone.

"We've got to get moving, kids. The way is clear for now, but I can't guarantee how long that'll last. That spacer we knocked out is going to be missed."

I waved her away. "Right. You folks get going. I'll stay with Pinky."

"We kinda need every hand on deck," Aylin insisted.

"I'm not leaving him!"

"Kitra," Sirena said softly. "I've got him. What you can do for Pinky is help get this ship back so we can take him to a place of better care."

I slid my hands along Pinky's rubbery side. It felt like desertion. But Sirena was right. And my other friends needed me, too. It was as much a matter of life or death for them as it was for him. Me, too, I remembered.

I put my hands in my pockets, licked my lips, and nodded.

"Right. Let's get going."

Chapter 13

"It's eerie," Marta whispered as we climbed the ladder toward Deck Five. "It's almost like being on a ghost ship, what with no one in the halls."

"Except for that one guy," I said distractedly. I was worried about leaving Sirena behind. That had cut our group down to just five. Sirena was a particularly bad one to lose. She was as fierce as anything; unarmed, she took down a guy wielding a beamer back on Purité. On the other hand, that had been out in the open, with three dimensions to maneuver in. And even then, his bolt had taken out her chair's antigrav, penetrating her shield. The memory of Sirena, sprawled and helpless on the floor of the chaff chamber, came back to me, and I gave a violent shudder.

In any event, it would have been a tight fit for her in the narrow accessway we were ascending through. That was a kind of providence, I guess.

Aylin waited for us at the top of the cylindrical shaft. There was enough room for her and Marta to stand on the little ledge on either side of the open door to the Deck Five passage. I waited on the ladder.

"You said auxiliary control is on this deck," I breathed. "It can't be too far away, so we should have a plan before we leave this cover. Tell us what we should expect. What exactly is this place we're taking?"

The spacer leaned back against the wall, crossing her arms and considering her words. "Alright. Here's how the control areas work. The bridge is what you'd expect. All the comms, engineering, armament controls go through there. It's pretty big because the *Faucon* sometimes leads a task force. So there could be up to a dozen people in there. Sensor CIC is the next biggest nerve center. You could technically run the ship from there. I expect that's fully crewed, too."

She tapped a finger against her sleeve. "Auxcon, on the other hand, is a failsafe. If the main ops centers get slagged from combat damage or whatever, the bridge functions are duplicated in there. It's almost like an appendix. We're trained to use it, but if we ever need it, things have to be pretty dire. It's cramped and kind of a kluge. It's kept dark during normal operations. There may not be anyone in there right now."

Marta dug into her belt pouch and pulled out…a compact of all things. Was she going to touch up her make-up before a fight? Then she popped it open and used the mirror to peer around the edge of the door, and I felt rather stupid.

"How far up the hall did you say the auxcon is?" she whispered.

"Just 15 meters or so."

She grimaced. "Well, they didn't leave it dark, then."

Aylin sagged slightly. "How many?"

Marta peered into her mirror, angling it slightly. "There are two people standing in front of a red door on the left…no, sorry…right side, about that far away."

"That's auxcon, alright. Are they armed?"

"Can't tell. They're wearing clothes like yours."

"Well, we'll have the drop on them, at least." She looked down at the squat pistol in her hand. "I can hit them with my gummer. That'll root them pretty good."

"They could still call for help," I objected.

"Then I'll trade with your friend." Aylin gestured to Fareedh. "Get me the stunner. But I want the gummer back afterwards."

"What's going on up there?" Fareedh whispered. I could barely make him out below Peter. He probably couldn't have heard our conversation. I took the gun from Aylin, passed it down to Peter. A moment later, he pressed a smaller weapon into my hand. It looked dark and ineffectual compared to the shiny beamers at Marta's hips. I offered it to Aylin.

"You'll have to get both of them quickly," I rasped. "Can you do it?"

"I'll try," she said. The spacer slid around to the edge of the door, exposing an eye and raising the stunner to firing position. I pulled the hypo from my hip belt again.

The pistol made a barely audible hum. A cry rang out from the corridor, followed by a slump, drowning out the stunner's next shots. Aylin stepped out into the passageway, looked keenly down the hall, then jerkily waved us out. The two guards Marta had seen were sprawled out on the deck. We quick-stepped to the door.

"How long will this last?" I asked Aylin.

"Depends on the person. Should be a fair bit."

The red door wasn't opening. With an, "Aha!", Aylin took the pass card from one of the sleeping guards and pressed it to the opening pad. The portal slid sideways. Air rushed out, smelling stale and metallic. Fareedh went in first, followed by Aylin. I started to move. My foot was stuck. I looked down.

One of the guards had his big hands around my boot. I yelped and fell on him, jabbing at his neck with my hypo and holding it there. He jerked once, then went limp.

"Let's get the other one," Peter said, looming over them. "Unless we can find something to truss her up."

"Let me see how much you've got left," Marta said, offering her palm. I handed her the hypo, and she made a little face. "Did you have to use the whole hypo?"

"I didn't know how much to use! Did I kill him?"

She peeled back an eyelid, felt at his neck for a pulse. "No, he's fine. At high concentrations, it just renders itself inert. Here. I'll do the next one."

The other guard, a young woman with short-cropped hair, didn't stir as Marta injected her.

"Let's bring them inside," Peter said to Marta. "Grab the legs?"

I quickly ducked into the auxcon to clear the way for them. Fareedh was already at one of the panels. I was struck by how small the room was. It didn't seem capable of controlling a big cruiser. There were only three stations, and some of the displays weren't even holographic.

"You're right," I said to Aylin. "This is pretty crude."

She nodded. "It's as simple as possible. Less stuff to break."

"Can you get into the ship's *sayar* from here?" I asked Fareedh.

He didn't look up. "Working on it. Trying to find the…there we go. Gravitics and environment."

Peter and Marta had finished hauling the sleeping guards in and had left them propped in sitting positions flanking the entrance. "Can you shut down the ship's weapons?" Peter asked.

"Not easily. They're decentralized. But I can give them plenty to worry about."

"Can't they just as easily turn everything back on?" I asked.

"Probably," Fareedh said. "I can stay here and try to stop it."

I had a vision of dueling programmers flicking off and on the lights and antigrav. "That'll be as bad for us as it is for them, if not worse. Anyway, we're already down to five. We can't afford to leave you behind."

He turned to look at me for the first time. "What do you have in mind?"

I considered. "Could you trigger a program remotely?" I asked.

Fareedh clicked his tongue against his teeth. "That deep, only from here."

"How about a time delay," Marta suggested. "Long enough for us to get into position. That would give your brother's team a schedule to work with, too."

"The problem is that someone on the bridge might notice it and reverse it." Fareedh's eyes got a faraway look. Then he nodded. "I'll have to work it in the back end. Let me see what failsafes would trigger a blackout or a grav loss."

I looked nervously at the sleeping guards. "How long will it take?"

"Longer if you bug me."

I left him alone. When Fareedh started snapping like Peter, he was really wound up.

My gaze wandered over the other panels, and the screens over them.

"Aylin," I said quietly. "Can you access the surveillance system?"

"Huh? Oh, sure, I think."

She sat down at one of the open seats, the panel lighting up automatically. The spacer searched through a few menus, finding what she wanted almost immediately. The display lit up with a small room, dimly lit, with three consoles and seats. Two of them were occupied: a tall, slim person in uniform with close-cropped hair and a shorter, stockier one in a space suit. She wore her long black hair in a ponytail.

I whirled around and saw the round port of a sensor. I pointed and squeaked, "Peter! Can you cover that up?"

"Oh crap." He fumbled in one of his tool pouches, producing a little cylinder, and lurched toward the sensor. A little hiss accompanied a gooey spray that spurted out onto the port.

"It's contact weld," he explained. "Not meant for this, but it'll do the job."

I looked back and saw the panel display had gone dark. That was better.

"You think anyone saw that?" Marta asked.

Peter cocked an ear, looking around. "I don't hear any alarms."

"Lord," I breathed. "If someone had been monitoring this room, we'd be cooked."

"Or maybe they already saw us, and they're waiting to see what we do," Peter said mock-cheerfully.

"Thanks," I said.

Marta ruffled his hair. "You're a 'fuel tank is always half empty' sorta guy," she said. Looking at me, she added, "Are you trying to get a view of the bridge?"

I nodded. "That's what I was hoping for."

"Let's see if they've thought to shut that off," Aylin said, sliding through menus again. There were at least four entries marked "bridge". She selected all of them, and the display expanded to a quartered view. One of them was dark in a muffled sort of way, as if there were a person seated or standing right in front. Another showed a forehead and dark crewcut, and beyond, a Window and the backs of at least three people in uniform. Yet another featured what looked like a recessed area with two angled walls radiating from a big door. It was closed and flanked by two tough types in full security rig.

The last view pointed straight at the captain's station. A rather nondescript man, balding and with a small dark mustache, stared straight ahead, presumably at the Window. Not at us, I hoped. He wore the stripes of a commander's rank.

"2nd Officer Akar," Aylin said as if the words didn't quite fit her mouth. "Well, that's a surprise."

"He doesn't look like much," Marta said.

"Akar came up from ops," Aylin said. "Ran the CiC. People liked him. He wasn't a hard-ass like Tinaz or the Captain. More the brainy type."

"I count eight on the bridge, including the guards," Marta said.

"That's not too bad, I guess," I replied.

Peter stepped toward the display. "What do you want to bet there's more in the halls on the way there? Excuse me." He reached past Aylin and began hunting for other displays.

"There're two main entrances to the bridge," the spacer said.

"You mean there are other ways in?" I asked.

"Yeah. There's a flag bridge above the main bridge, for when we have admirals or commodores leading a task force. It's normally not in use." She looked up at Peter, a trace of annoyance on her face. He still hadn't found sensors for the hallways going to the bridge.

"Sorry," he said, stepping back. Aylin spotted the flag bridge monitor pretty quick and called it up. The room was dark, faintly outlined in the glow of unattended panels. It seemed strangely cramped, as if the deck had been built too high.

Marta said. "How hard would it be to get in there?"

"It's gold braid country," the spacer replied. "Secure when occupied. Locked otherwise." Her sharp-lined face took on a speculative look. "But without your friend in her big scooter..." She called up a schematic of the long ship, zooming in on a spot amidships near the dorsal edge. "There's a battery on Deck One. That'll be crewed and guarded. But there's accessways underneath, for maintenance. We could get into that system...here." She pointed at a spot one deck up from the auxcon, just starboard of where we were.

"So we *are* crawling through air vents," I said, shaking my head slightly.

A smile curved Aylin's thin lips. "Gotta fix things somehow. I'm not saying it won't be a tight fit." She looked up at Marta and Peter. "Especially for you two."

"We'll plot that course when we come to it," Peter said. "If anything, we'll—"

"Folks, I've got something," Fareedh called quietly from his station.

We were crammed at his side in nothing flat.

The programmer gave us a canny smile and an eyebrow wriggle. "Do you want to hear of my genius, or is it just enough to give you a time frame?"

Peter folded his arms. "Could we keep you from bragging?"

"Not likely, but we are pressed for time."

"Well, *I* want to hear what's up," Aylin said. "If we're sticking our heads in the noose, I at least want to make sure all the curves are squared."

Fareedh nodded. "Fair enough. Okay, long story short, I looked for the triggers for a soft shutdown. We don't want the *Faucon* going so dark we can't get it going again. We don't want the air going off, either. That meant I couldn't hit the power plant directly. But I did find this little guy…"

He pointed to a glowing box among many boxes on a display. It didn't mean anything to me, nor the gibberish of characters in a connected subdisplay.

"Exactly twenty minutes from when you tell me, this coolant regulator is going to think it's off-line. As a precaution, it's going to shut down the cooling subsystem. That'll trigger a standby shutdown of the plant."

"That sounds…bad?" I said.

"Not so bad. The plasma containment will stay online, but the fuel will stop going in. It should shut down everything nonessential to keep the batteries from draining too fast. The plant will stay warm in the meantime."

"That sounds perfect!" Marta said, giving Fareedh's shoulder a squeeze. "How long will it last?"

Fareedh cocked his head in a shrug. "Until they replace the regulator. Or run a system diagnostic and find my routine. It won't be hidden. Best I can do in the next ten minutes. If you want to stay here longer…"

"Sure," Peter said. "Because it's so cozy in here. No chance they'll follow up on that guard we knocked out."

"That's what I figured. Alright. Quiet again for the maestro." He raised his hands dramatically, then set to his coding.

We let him be in a silence that stretched. My head whirled, a jumble of competing worries. Pinky. The *Majera* floating pilotless in space. What was going on down on Hyvilma. I thought about getting up to pace, but I didn't want to disturb Fareedh's programming. So, I closed my eyes and did the trick my therapist taught me when I was eleven. Deep breath. Inhale four seconds, hold for three, out for seven. Again. And again.

The shards of concern sort of melted, leaving calm black. I opened my eyes, and I felt like I could focus again.

"Seven minutes," Fareedh said, savoring the words in satisfaction. "Not bad if I do say so myself."

I smiled at him, then looked up at Aylin.

"To the air vents?"

She gave a quiet snort, then nodded. "To the air vents."

Chapter 14

Arm over arm, I clambered in the near-darkness, the crazily dancing light of Aylin's torch doing little more than occasionally dazzling me. It was close and musty inside the accessway, but not too hard to maneuver. The same smallness that made me a good match for a cramped glider cockpit was serving me well here. Fareedh and Aylin weren't small, but they were long rather than wide. She'd *allez-ooped* into the ceiling without touching the sides, and while I couldn't see Fareedh, crawling at the rear, I was pretty sure he was alright, limber as he was. Peter and Marta, on the other hand…

I could hear them behind me, Marta breathing heavily as she brushed the walls with every move. More than once, I heard a spate of quiet creative cursing from Peter as he bumped against a carelessly dogged hatch, projecting invisibly into the smooth crawlway.

I was just glad none of us were claustrophobic.

How much longer did we have? I'd checked my *sayar* before we'd gone through the hatch into the ceiling. This passage was like an endless treadmill, the monotony broken only by a few cross passages and smudges of sprayed-on text. We might have been inside five minutes or maybe ten. And it had taken us six minutes to get there, two minutes longer than it should have, thanks to two spacers patrolling the deck. But I couldn't stop, and I couldn't easily check the time. No point worrying over things I couldn't control, I thought. The sweat kept dripping and my stomach kept roiling anyway.

At last, Aylin stopped. I panted while she checked her *sayar*. Then she gave me the thumbs up and began fiddling with the deck in front of her. It hinged open suddenly, dim light turning the spacer's face into a ghost's profile. She was able to get her legs under her with near-contortionist skill, then dropped into the room feet first. I braced for the sound of guns or a cry of alarm.

Instead, I heard a light scuff, as if something were being dragged on carpet. A few moments later, Aylin's face popped up into the crawlway, shadows making her grin look like that of a ghoul.

"All good," she whispered. "Come on down."

It wasn't as easy for me to uncoil. I got wrapped up in a little ball and found I couldn't get my cramped legs in front of me. So I just sort of tumbled back, curled knees bumping the top of the passage. I barely made out Marta's upside-down smiling face, torchlight glinting off her eyes. I was able to kick my legs in front of me though and scoot myself forward like an inchworm until my feet found empty space. I had just enough room to crouch in a sitting position. There were a couple of big boxes conveniently sited just a meter under the hatch. Aylin must have moved them there. I hopped down, the spacer bracing me for a soft landing.

I looked up at the panel in the ceiling. Marta's face appeared. "I can't turn around!" she breathed.

"Just dive through," Aylin called quietly. "We'll catch you."

I looked doubtfully at the spacer. Marta and Peter both massed more than 100 kilos. Marta was already coming through like a newborn from her mom, though. We both took a shoulder and heaved up until her hands were on the box right under the hatch. Then we were bracing her hips and legs as she did walking pushups onto the other nearby box. She rolled over, hopped with remarkable grace to the floor, and threw out her arms.

"Ta-dah!" she said quietly.

I smiled at that, then found myself suppressing a giggle with the back of my hand. Marta was positively grimy with dust and grease from head to toe. She looked like an old-style camouflaged soldier. Well, that probably wasn't a bad thing, but she'd die if she saw herself like this.

Before Marta could ask what was so funny, Peter was already emerging from the ceiling, and Marta was helping him down. Unassisted. Once he was on the deck, it was clear he'd rubbed against as much *schmutz* as Marta.

Fareedh came last, feet first and virtually spotless, as if this were part of his everyday regimen.

"What's with all the cargo?" he asked, looking around the cramped room. I realized now why the deck had looked so high on the monitor. Most of the floor was taken up with boxes. I torched my *sayar* to shine on the nearest one. *Cheese Concentrate, Thermostabilized.* The next one over said *Pideh, Dehydrated.* A third was *Chickpeas, Irradiated.* That sounded tasty.

"Is this normal?" I asked Aylin. "All the food?"

"Not usually," she said. "When we're in orbit, we get fresh food from Hyvilma in regular shipments. We only fill the unused rooms when we're planning to do a long patrol. I don't even remember these being loaded. Iskender might know."

So that's why the deck here was so full of stuff. The implications were frightening. Was the *Faucon* planning on going off on a private raiding mission? With its range, the cruiser could Jump back across the Rift and start a spree. But if that were the case, why hadn't they left already?

My heart sank. Maybe the revolt was happening on the other side of the Rift, too, and the *Faucon* was just waiting for reinforcements or relief. Yet another reason to hurry.

"Did you fill your brother in on the plan?" I asked Fareedh.

"Yeah, on our way out. He knows the power's going out and we're trying for the bridge."

I made my way around the boxes to find the downstairs hatch. It was hard to get my bearings with everything so crowded and covered.

"Can someone help me find the way down?" I whispered hoarsely. "I want to be ready when the lights go off."

Fareedh made a quick surveying look of the room, then started off through the boxes in almost the opposite direction I was going. So much for my pilot's sense of direction.

He pointed down, turned and gave us a thumbs up. I blew out a breath and sat on the nearest box.

"I guess we just wait, then." I fumbled for my *sayar* to check the time. The hissing sound of an irising portal caused me to drop the device with a clatter, random displays floating crazily a meter above. I whirled toward Fareedh. He was also turning around...

...to face directly into the mouth of a pistol.

One of the goons I'd seen guarding the bridge door, or maybe there were more I had missed, ascended the ladder, gun outstretched. It was an ugly little thing, nothing at all like the sleek stunner or the thick gummer.

"What the hell are you doing up here?" the spacer called in a low, slightly muffled masculine voice. His face was obscured by an opaque screen, but I could tell he was looking Fareedh up and down.

"Ah, sir, just checking supplies, sir," Fareedh managed with admirable calm. "Lieutenant Konak sent me."

"Konak, huh? You always work in the dark?" The spacer was illuminated from below, currently the brightest thing in the room. I sat very still and tried not to breathe.

Before Fareedh could answer, the guard had torched his gun to play a light on Fareedh, the oversized tunic contrasting sharply with his uncovered suit bottoms.

"Where's your trousers, spacer?"

"I..."

Fareedh was cut off by a loud buzzing sound, and he jack-knifed, falling to the floor.

I looked on, stunned.

"You son of a *bitch*," Peter roared, launching himself past me at the guard. There was another buzzing whine, but if Peter was hit, I couldn't tell. I rushed forward to do something, anything.

At the base of one of the consoles on one of the few bare patches of deck, I dimly saw Peter with the guard's neck vised in an elbow. Peter grunted, tightened his grip, and the gun clattered to the floor. I turned to Fareedh and knelt at his side. He was curled up next to a box, shuddering, arms wrapped around his middle. I reached for him, and then my fingers were sticky and dark.

I froze, staring at my blood-black hands.

"Kitra," Fareedh breathed. I heard bubbles in his voice. I looked down, saw his face distorted with pain. He was staring at the stunner at his hip, the one he'd loaned to Aylin before.

The world went crystalline clear, sound fading away. I unsnapped the gun from Fareedh's belt, pressed it to the struggling guard's temple, and fired. Nothing. I shrieked in animal rage, running my fingers over the smooth plastic, looking for a safety, or whatever might be keeping the damned thing from working. Something gave way under my thumb, and I pointed the weapon again. I knew firing a stunner this close might kill the man. I didn't care.

I fired. My eardrums fluttered, and the guard was suddenly limp in Peter's grip. With his struggling suddenly ceased, Peter fell backward, the unconscious or dead guard unfolding back with him. Peter breathed heavily.

"Get that hatch closed!" Aylin called.

"Fareedh's hit!" I yelled back, jerking for the hatch. Behind me, I sensed rather than saw Marta making her way toward us. Before I could get to the portal, another suited spacer was coming through. They already had an arm hooked over the lip of the hatch. Then, with seeming slowness, a figure rose up from the portal and swung their other hand around. Something dark and pointed came into view with me as the target. At this range, it couldn't miss. My stunner, limp at my side, seemed a light year away. It was a race I was going to lose.

A lance of heat sizzled past me, leaving the stench of scorched meat in my nostrils. I looked down in horror, but saw no holes or burns. I looked back up to find the armed spacer crumpling to the ground, their chest a ruin of charred cloth and armor plastic. Marta charged forward to my right, beamers in both hands. She wasn't headed toward the guard she'd shot, but working her way toward Fareedh, kicking full boxes out of the way as she went. I turned to join her, realized I needed to stay covering the hatch, and found myself doing a complete revolution in the air.

I looked down in panic and saw my feet rising off the deck. An alarm tore through the room, a discordant, punctuated klaxon. The light from the open hatch dimmed to a sullen red. I flailed until I hit the ceiling, then bounced back to the deck amidst a pile of floating boxes. It was impossible to see half a meter in front of me for all the drifting cargo. At last, I thought to magnetize my boots, and they clamped me firmly. Now that I had a *down* again, I was able to move forward, step by deliberate step, pushing the cartons aside as I went.

Just in time to see a third spacer, this one a woman in an officer's tunic, struggling to dog the hatch as Aylin tugged in the opposite direction. Our ally wasn't trying to close our room off anymore, but to keep the passage clear to assault the bridge. The intruder saw me coming and fired a bolt. The container floating between her and me exploded in a flower of pâté, droplets of steamy liver spattering my face. I fired back with the stunner, trying not to hit Aylin. My ears tingled as the shot went wide, harmless.

But the officer didn't get a chance to fire again. Peter was on her, hooking his feet into the hinge of the hatch and flinging her across the room. She sailed past me, knocking cartons aside willy-nilly. I got a second shot off, and she thumped bonelessly against a raised console.

Now what? We couldn't stay up here. Even with the power outage, if we didn't distract them, the mutineers might be able to seal off the passageways, cut off the air, or worse. Iskender and his people would be mowed down before they could get anywhere.

"We're going in," I whispered to Aylin between peals of the alarm.

"Me too," Marta said, but she looked uncertainly back down at Fareedh. His head was cradled in her arms, and she was applying pressure to a bandage.

"Fareedh needs you. We'll be alright. Aylin, you get off a gummer shot, and I'll be right behind you."

The spacer waved a salute at me and crouched by the door. I clomped next to her. There was no one at the hatch or down the ladder below. Who knew what was perched just outside our field of vision, though. Aylin unmagged her boots and sprang down the hole, firing as she went. I switched off my mags, mouthed a prayer, and jumped after her before my hindbrain could stop me from such foolishness.

A whirlwind of images met my eyes as I plunged: consoles and displays flashing; red low-power lights gleaming from the ceiling; two men spread-eagle against their panels struggling against constricting gray filaments; the man I'd seen in the captain's chair leveling a gun at me.

A low whine buzzed my inner ears and I felt my legs go numb. I managed to wriggle around and fire a wild shot. The commander's hand flung open nervelessly, the weapon flying from his grip. Then my back hit the deck and I bounced up again. Aylin had already magged down her boots and was shooting her gummer like a firehose. That took out two more, wrapped together like twin bugs in a cocoon. For good measure, she sprayed the doors.

I didn't want to look at my legs. I was sure they'd been burned to stumps, only shock keeping them from blinding me with pain. Something drifted by me, and I plucked it out of the air instinctively. A stunner, inlaid with faux brown wood. That was what I'd shot out of Akar's hand, I realized. And that gave me the courage to look down. Sure enough, my legs were unmarked, seemingly unharmed.

I magged my boots to keep from bouncing around the room. There I stood, sort of, swaying on my sleeping legs, with two stunners leveled at the leader of the mutineers.

He relaxed into his chair and smiled ruefully.

"Maybe we can talk this over," he said.

"What's there to talk about?" Aylin barked. "Give us our ship back."

Akar made to face her, looked at my guns, then thought better of it. Instead, he addressed me.

"If you want to split hairs, I'm the senior officer. You're the ones leading the mutiny."

I scoffed. "Yeah? Where's the captain?"

The commander took on a pained expression. "She didn't see eye to eye with us."

"So you murdered her?" I said with acid.

His eyes showed surprise. "We certainly did not."

"Never mind that," I said. "Aylin, how is Iskender's group doing? We've got to get a doctor here fast for Fareedh."

She had to go to the far side of the bridge to find a panel that didn't have a gummed mutineer stuck to it. Her sharp face broke into a scowl. "There's a firefight going on in the pinnace bay. I can't tell who's winning. A bunch of people are floating, knocked out or dead."

"This is madness," Akar said urgently. "No one else should have to get hurt. We should be working together, not fighting."

"What, and join your pirate fleet?" I bit out.

"I promise you, the last thing we are is pirates."

He shifted in his chair, resting his good elbow and looking less like a mutineer and more like my 9th grade civics teacher. I'd liked him.

Then he waved his good hand. My finger tightened on the stunner's trigger for a moment, but he was just gesturing. "This cruiser," he went on. "It wasn't stationed here to protect the Frontier. At least, not its people. Its sole purpose is to keep the planets in line. To smash any colony that doesn't toe the line." His dark eyes looked at me entreatingly. "The *Faucon* isn't an instrument of protection. It's a bloody police club."

"That's ridiculous," I said. "And anyway, I can tell you some places that could use a bit of policing." I was thinking of the Puritans. I still stung at the thought of them, how they'd ambushed us and almost stole *Majera* from us.

He frowned, his features taking on a note of concern. "You're very young."

"What difference does that make?"

He leaned forward. "You might think differently if you'd seen what I have. I'm 65. I remember the Talvi subjugations. I was there"

They'd been covered in school, briefly. I shook my head impatiently. "So what?"

"Ask the Talvans if Imperial pacification is some theoretical concept. A long-forgotten episode like the suppression of Finitism." His eyes flashed as he added quietly. "It's still going on."

I heard footsteps cautiously coming down the ladder, boot by magnetic boot. He looked up. "Ask your friend there about Imperial suppression. I'll wager his family goes back to Äärettömyys."

Peter's voice shot back, "Yeah. And I'd have a lot more sympathy for your cause if you *hadn't just shot my best friend.*" I heard a thunk as his boots hit the deck. He walked into view, hulking over the commander. His face, where it showed under the grime, was red with fury. "You've killed and you're still killing. I've had enough of it."

"What can we do to help Iskender?" I asked, relieved at the interruption.

Aylin shrugged her thin shoulders. "Your friend locked the system pretty good. I can run the diagnostic, but it'll take a good twenty minutes to cycle through. I'm not a *sayar* slinger." She looked at Peter. "You're an engineer, yeah?"

"Sure. On a 200-ton scout."

"What's a couple of orders of magnitudes between friends? Help me out."

"*Kaaoksen perkelen,*" he muttered, something he saved for rare occasions. He shoved the solo gummed spacer aside from her panel. She floated away, struggling feebly, until she came in contact with the ceiling and stuck like a spider's egg to a web. Peter fiddled with displays a moment, grunted, and said, "Okay, I've got access. But there's no way I can fire the engines without help. I don't know the first thing about internal security protocols either. If only Fareedh…" His hand curled into a fist, and his broad back started to shake.

"Easy," I said. "Let's focus on what we can do." I had an idea. "You. Commander. Go on the shipwides and tell your people to stand down."

His eyes widened slightly, and he shook his head. "I can't do that."

"Look," I went on. "The Navy's going to send another ship here sooner or later. Even if you win the fight, you won't have enough crew to run this cruiser. Give up now before more people get hurt."

His eyes flickered to the Window, then leveled on mine. He was silent long enough that the zero-gee klaxon sounded once before he spoke. "If you want the fighting to stop, ask your people to stand down. I promise clemency for everyone. We can drop them off on Hyvilma." His eyes softened. "You're in over your head. This is much bigger than you realize. Do you think we'd have started this if it were just us?"

Sweat prickled beneath my suit.

"You're bluffing," I said.

He leaned back with a sigh and was silent. But he looked fixedly at me, challenging my assertion without words.

Son of a bitch. How far did this rebellion go? I had visions of Sennet blockaded by their own ships, of a movement spanning the whole Frontier. No wonder he was so calm. Relaxed in his chair without a bead of sweat on his high forehead, even with his cohorts bound and helpless. I was the one holding the gun, and it might as well have been a toothpick. This was way more than I could handle. I was a tiny person in a galaxy-wide event.

I shook my head. None of that mattered. What mattered was Pinky and Fareedh seeing a doctor. What mattered was Iskender not being one of the floating bodies on the monitor.

"Aylin, open the shipwide comms, please," I said, smooth as glass.

Chapter 15

She blinked at me, then a smile tugged at her lips. The tech turned to a panel and fiddled. A moment later, she waved. "You're on."

I licked my lips. It's not like I'd prepared a speech. But the words came out anyway.

"This is Captain Yilmaz addressing all hands from the bridge. All rebellious troops, lay down your arms at once, by order of the Governor of Sennet and the Imperial Trans Frontier authority." I put as much flint as I could into the words. My mother was my model. I remembered how she'd addressed politicians, union leaders, huge crowds with complete calm and control.

Peter's eyes bugged. I didn't bother to look at Akar.

"We have Commander Akar and the bridge mutineers confined. The ship is under Imperial control. Lay down your arms, and we will listen sympathetically to your case. If you continue to fight, we will assume you are all as responsible as the 2nd Officer." I swallowed. "There is one punishment for mutiny."

I didn't actually know what the punishment for mutiny was. It was death in the space adventures I read. I didn't want any more people to die, though. Not even Akar.

I waved my hand in what I hoped Aylin would recognize as the cut-comms gesture. She did.

"How's it looking?" I asked her.

"Still fighting," she said. "Though it seems less fierce. Yeah. One of Iskender's groups just made it across to Armory D. No one shot at them."

It was working! I smiled and raised my hand to get the comms going again. Before I'd completed the gesture, there was a harsh thumping on the door. I jumped in my shoes, nearly spraining my ankles; my boots kept me stuck to the deck. At least my legs were working again.

"They're trying to get in!" Peter said, pointing at the half-gummed door. The portal whirred as it strained against the sticky strands.

"Seal it, Aylin!" I shouted.

"Out of charge," she called back.

The door slid half open. I caught a glimpse of an arm hooking around, then another holding a gun. I unmagged and launched upward to cling to a ceiling hold and crouch there. Pins and needles went through my legs as they came back to life. The armored intruder ducked under the solidified gum and began making his way in, pushing the stuck door aside.

"Peter, do something!"

"I can't! I'm locked out of the antigrav, and I can't...waitaminute." His hands flashed across his console.

Something slammed me, swinging me like a pendulum and wrenching my left arm. I barely managed to keep my grip on the ceiling handhold. The intruder sailed past me in a tumble, and I fired once, twice, my ears ringing with the shots. He stopped flailing and thumped hard against the far wall. He bounced, drifting back more slowly. He wasn't moving anymore.

"Jets!" Peter yelled like a victory cry.

"What?" The word didn't make any sense.

"The back-up maneuvering jets aren't part of the shut down system. We don't have them on *Majera*, but *Faucon's* got 'em. Gave the ship a nice jolt." He grinned fiercely. "Want me to hit 'em again?"

"Hold on a sec," I said. I went back to the deck and magged my boots. I needed the orientation or I got dizzy. Akar looked a little sick in his chair, no longer the picture of self-confidence. He must have gotten thrown against his straps pretty hard.

"Hook me up again, Aylin," I called.

"You got it."

I took a deep breath. "Attention all hands on the *Faucon*. This is Captain Yilmaz. We have complete control of the vessel. If the..." I paused a split second to choose my words, "...crew acting under Commander Akar's orders do not stand down, we will take drastic measures. Including selective engagement of the antigrav system."

Peter laughed at that one, a little explosion of air. Sure, it was a bluff, but I couldn't imagine any of the mutineers would want to bet against me and risk being pinned at several gees to the floor.

"Kitra!" Aylin called. "A whole squad just flung aside their guns. One of our teams is rounding them up!"

"Thank goodness," I breathed.

"We're getting a comm from Lieutenant Konak," the spacer added.

"Cut the shipwides and make Iskender's live," I said.

The tenor voice of Fareedh's brother filled the bridge. "Aft section secure," he said breathlessly. "Kitra, are you really up there?"

"Sure am, Iskender! Everyone but Pinky and Sirena, who we left in sick bay." I hoped Pinky hadn't been thrown around too much. For that matter, I hoped Fareedh was okay. A squirt of acid swirled in my belly.

"We're making our way to you. Resistance seems to have stopped. What should we do now?"

"Uhhhh…" I looked at Akar. "You said you didn't kill the captain. Where are they?"

The commander was staring off into space, looking as if he hadn't heard me. I followed his gaze and saw he was looking at a chronometer display. He turned his eyes from it, smiled weakly, and said, "She's asleep. She'll be asleep for a good long while."

"You *did* kill her," Peter growled, taking a step from his console.

"I did not, you idiot. She's sedated." One of the corners of his mouth quirked. "The *Faucon's* senior officer, such as it is, is your quartermaster friend."

I was still processing Akar's actions, not his words. If he was watching the clock, it meant he was expecting something soon. Was he waiting for the ship's systems to come online? I couldn't see what good that would do him, not with us in control. Reinforcements? Those could only come from two places: the planet, and from Jump. A chill came on me as I thought about Akar's cryptic words. If another rebel ship was on its way, we had to have *Faucon* back in action as soon as possible. Which meant we needed a skipper.

"Lieutenant Konak," I called out. "Please report to the bridge."

The color leached from under the freckles on Iskender's cheeks. He swallowed, but managed to say in a firm voice, "Are you sure?"

I pointed at Akar, now pressed between two of Iskender's crew with hands bound behind him. "That's what he says."

"Where's the skipper?" Fareedh's brother asked.

"Forward brig," he answered curtly.

"And Commander Tinaz?"

At that, the mustached prisoner's eyes shifted away. He didn't answer.

"Well?"

"The morgue."

I blurted, "But you said…"

Wrinkles seamed his forehead, and he seemed to sag. "It wasn't the plan. Some of us have differing opinions on methods."

Peter stepped toward him with balled fists. "Is that why you're packing lethal weapons?"

Akar didn't answer.

"There are," Iskender said, then hesitated a moment before continuing, "three other Lieutenants senior to me. First Lieutenant Ghazali was the one who locked us up. And I saw Lieutenant Pahlavi go down in the corridors. What happened to Predescu?"

One of the two spacers Aylin had gummed into a grotesque embrace at their bridge station spat out, "He tried to stick up for Tinaz. I was happy to get both of those martinets."

"I promise you," Akar began. "It was not the intent…"

There was no lack of color in Iskender's cheeks now. "Right now, I don't care." He waved at the spacers restraining Akar. "Take him to the forward brig and check on the captain. Take a medic, and see if she can't be roused. If it's more serious, the Doc can see to her after they're finished patching up my brother."

The pair saluted and hauled the head mutineer away. That left half a dozen of the team he'd brought with him.

"How much longer 'till gravity's back?" he asked Aylin.

She checked her panel. "About three minutes."

"Kill that, would you?" Iskender called. I looked at him in confusion until I realized he was talking about the emergency alarm. It had been going so long, it was almost background noise.

"Aye, aye, supe," Aylin replied.

He waited a moment, then visibly relaxed when the klaxon didn't blare again. He looked at his crewmates and pointed at the three gummed spacers and the unconscious guard currently floating near the ceiling. "You folks, get rid of these four, too. You should be able to make larboard brig before we have gees again."

There were salutes and then a brief bustle as the spacers tugged the floating prisoners away like so many bundles of cargo. Just one of the team stayed behind, a tough-looking man who kept his stunner unslung and watched the half-gummed open portal.

Iskender ran a hand through his mussed, sandy hair. Then he unmagged and flew to the captain's chair with a grace that matched Fareedh's. He strapped himself in and dialed a private comm.

"Isra? How are things larboard side?"

The answer came quickly. "Wrapped up, Lieutenant," said a brisk high-register voice

"We need a full security detail at both ends of the ship, working their way inward. Akar's group don't all play by the same rules. Some might not have surrendered. I'm worried about saboteurs."

"Aye, aye, supe."

"And Isra, armor up. We don't need to lose any more of us, and they're going to be cornered rats."

A short pause. "Got it. We'll check in at initiation of the sweep."

Iskender closed the comms and looked at me. "You said another rebel ship could be coming in?"

I nodded. "I don't know for sure, but it looks like it, from what Akar said, and how he was acting."

"That's good enough for me." He pursed his lips. Then he eyed his armrest panel and tapped it. A new klaxon filled the bridge and the decks beyond, warbling up and then down. The lieutenant hit the shipwides and announced, "All hands, general quarters. Prepare for combat."

Chapter 16

Iskender looked up at me. "How long do you figure until reinforcements show up?"

"No idea. But it seemed like soon."

He nodded and eyed the Window a moment. I turned to see what he was looking at. The view still showed a map of planet Hyvilma's surroundings, with scattered glittering points representing the stranded orbital traffic.

"At least we'll see them if they pop in. We'll have the drop on them," he said. "Why don't you check up on Fareedh and then take him to sick bay." He smiled slightly. "My brother's talked a lot about you, you know."

I felt my cheeks flush. "Yeah, well, we've been flying together for a while."

His grin broadened, and he waggled his fair eyebrows in *exactly* the same way as his brother. "Sounded more serious than that."

I looked down at the deck. "We…sort of decided not to mix adventure with dating."

Iskender's voice softened a bit. "That's too bad. I don't see how he could do better."

Peter chuckled. "Plenty of fish in the sea, Iskender." He caught my eye and added, "Not that our Kitra isn't pretty amazing."

"Okay," I said, clumping toward the ladder. "If I stay here much longer, my head won't fit through the hatch."

At the ladder, I braced for a jump, then decided against it. If the gravity came on mid flight, that would be bad. Instead, I carefully arm-over-armed it. But halfway up, I paused. Something was nagging at me.

"What's up, Kitra?" Iskender asked, looking up at me.

"You said we'd have the drop on a rebel when it Jumped in."

He frowned slightly. "Yeah. Am I wrong?"

"What if they're already here?"

Peter slapped his forehead. "Infinity. Without transponders, like us. That would explain why Akar was looking so intently at the screen. He was looking for a buddy. It'd be too much coincidence, even for me, if another ship just happened to come out of hyperspace the moment we took over the *Faucon*." He smiled weakly.

"Skipper, check the conn logs for comms from the skipper seat," Aylin called sharply from her station.

Iskender fumbled with the *sayar* in the captain's chair until he found what he was looking for. His eyes widened.

"Lord, you're right," he breathed.

"A message?" Aylin asked.

Iskender nodded. "Yah. From the time code, right before I got here. He must have sent it when you weren't looking."

I bristled. "I was watching him the whole time!"

He flapped his palms. "Then maybe he sent it subvocally or something. The point is, he signaled another ship."

Peter's voice quavered slightly, "Maybe he was contacting Hyvilma?"

The lieutenant shook his head. "It's point-to-point. The destination isn't the planet." His forehead unfurrowed. "Ah, but now we know where they are. At least in what direction. Alright, signal an orbital plane change. 15 degrees."

There was silence. Iskender swiveled his chair to look at Peter.

Peter looked at him blankly. "Um, what?"

"That's where you relay my orders to the engineering and navigation crew," Iskender explained.

"Yeah," Peter said flatly, "Iskender, I'm not a Navy officer. I don't know how to do that."

"Lord," the lieutenant said again. He punched the shipwides. "Ensigns Arslan and Tekin to the bridge, please. Immediately." He looked up at Peter. "Sorry. This is my first time."

"Hey, man. Me too."

"Why don't you go with Kitra? Aylin, can you take Peter's spot until the officers get here?"

"I can try," the spacer said.

"At least get eyes on this azimuth," Iskender said, tapping at his chair display. "This is where Akar was sending to." He turned to me. "Get moving, you two."

The spacer tending Fareedh was on the older side, with commander's stripes, short salt-and-pepper hair, and a warm, round face. They'd opened Fareedh's stolen tunic and cut away part of his space suit. The fabric was dark with blood, but the wound itself was glossy with emergency skin. Marta floated next to him, clasping one of his hands. His dark face looked like it had been dusted in chalk. But he smiled at me, blinking long-lashed eyes.

"The Doc here's good at their job," he breathed, wincing with the effort.

"How is he?" I asked the spacer.

Before the doctor could answer, Peter flew past me and clung to the panel that Fareedh was sort of wedged against. "Thank the cosmos, you're okay," he said, gingerly putting the other palm on Fareedh's shoulder. "We gotta get you out of here, pal. Fireworks are about to start."

"Peter!" Marta exclaimed, and then the two of them were twirling in spinning, weightless embrace. I sprang back to dodge them with a little too much effort and ended up airborne, sailing over the box-strewn deck. I flailed, grasping for any kind of handhold.

And promptly fell on top of a box of rice, which split at its seams under my weight. I got to my hands and knees, looked up. Peter and Marta were a tangle between two big packages struggling to extricate themselves. I looked for Fareedh and sighed with relief. The doctor had had quick reflexes, cradling their patient to prevent a fall.

"Grav's back on," I said superfluously.

"You don't say," they replied in a flat, mid-range voice. They cleared their throat. "Anyway, your friend will be fine, but he's lost a lot of blood, and he needs a transfusion." The doctor looked at Marta with twinkling eyes as she picked herself up. "If you can help me get him onto the stretcher, we can head for the sick bay."

Fareedh mumbled, "I wanna see Pinky."

The doctor looked confused. "Who's Pinky?" they asked me.

"Friend of ours. He's in the larboard sick bay."

The commander shook their head. "Main sick bay's closer and better appointed." They grasped Fareedh's shoulders as Marta took his legs and gently hoisted him onto a thin floating bed. "Don't worry," the doctor said softly. "You'll be just fine."

"No sweat, doc," Fareedh said with a languid wave followed by a wince. "Whatcher name anyhow?"

"Marku," they said offhandedly. The doctor navigated the boxes, pulling Fareedh on his stretcher with ease. They pulled flexible straps over him to keep him in place, and, stretcher in tow, went through a door. I suppressed a chuckle. What with all the going through the ceiling and floor hatches, I'd half believed the room didn't *have* a deck-level portal.

Marta grabbed my hand and squeezed as we went into the hall. "Don't think you'll get away without a hug, too. My big hero."

"Big doofus, you mean. Anyway, you're the one blasting away with two guns like something out of a Centauri show." Still, I kept her hand clasped in mine as we raced down the corridor. It was reassuring. And…familiar. Our fingers knit together automatically. It was kind of remarkable how well they fit given hers were half again as big as mine.

"Thank you for—" I started. Iskender's voice, blaring from every comm on the deck, interrupted.

"All hands, this is acting-Captain Konak. We have identified a destroyer-class vessel in wide orbit around Hyvilma. It is flying without transponder, and it has just made a course-changing burn. We must assume at this point that it is commanded by hostiles. All hands to battlestations."

The doctor stopped at a lift, palmed it open, and pulled Fareedh's sled inside. There was just enough room for all of us. Iskender's voice continued over the comms inside, his tone more hesitant.

"There is the possibility that there are spacers on board that ship who are being held prisoner, as we were." His voice strengthened again. *"We will do what we can to disable rather than destroy. But we must put the safety of the* Faucon, *and Hyvilma first."*

The lift doors opened on a new deck. Marku went out first into a huge corridor.

"Godspeed, and do your best, for Captain Sirocco, for Hyvilma, and for the Empire."

I looked at Fareedh's tousle-haired head and smiled. His brother was doing great. I'd had my doubts, but he'd taken the responsibility of command without flinching. I just hoped he could run the ship in combat, especially with a good portion of his crew out of action.

"How much further, Doc?" Peter asked. The corridor went on for dozens of meters, but we'd just passed a compartment blast door, the kind that closes in the event of decompression to seal off a section. The edges of its frame intruded nearly a full meter into the passageway.

"It's right down the hall, just after the amidships batter…"

A lance of light shot out from ahead, spearing Marku directly in the chest. They fell to the deck in a heap. Instinctively, I grabbed Fareedh's sled and yanked, dragging him back behind the lip of the blast door frame. Another shot sizzled by, and Marta tumbled in behind me. I smelled burnt hair. I looked at her in horror, but she stood up, unhurt and seemingly unaware of her singed curls. Peter had made it to cover behind the blast door frame on the other side of the hall, his grease-streaked face pale. The doctor lay still on the deck, arms flung out and eyes staring ahead unseeingly. My stomach pitched violently, and I grasped at Fareedh's sled to keep standing.

"Kitra, what do we do?" Peter yelled.

"We've got to get out of here!" I shouted back. But how? And where would we go? Fareedh needed help *now*, and I had no idea how to get to the other sick bays from here. Not without a map. I reached for my *sayar*. Maybe Peter could transfer the schematic from his *sayar*. My hand clutched air.

Gone! It wasn't at my hip!

Iskender's voice came over the comms again. *"Destroyer is closing quickly. All batteries, prepare to fire. Target power planet and armaments. Deploy chaff. Begin evasive maneuvers."* The ever present, almost subsonic thrum of the ship became an audible hum as the gravitics compensated for the *Faucon's* sudden thrust.

"I'm going to see what's going on," Marta hissed, pulling out her compact again. No sooner had she angled it around the jamb of the blast door than another bolt sliced through the air, blasting it from her hand. She squeaked and quickly retreated.

"The second we show our faces, we're dead," Peter groaned.

"All batteries, fire on my mark. Three, two, one, mark."

A pulse ran through the ship, a tremor that vibrated the deck and walls. A moment later, Iskender's voice came back on the comms.

"Amidships and larboard batteries, respond. Why aren't you firing?"

Nothing followed that. I wondered if he'd meant to send that directly rather than on the shipwides. Another shot came through the hall. Now they didn't even care about targets. They just wanted the hall clear.

I felt my gloved fingers curl in and rub against each other. Knowing the way back wasn't going to do us any good. We'd get drilled down the second we left the safety of the blast door frame. We needed help to get out of this fix. I didn't have a *sayar*. Oh, but Fareedh did! And it had a direct line to Iskender. There it was, still on his belt. I grabbed it and palmed frantically for the right display. There were a million of them on his *sayar*, all stacked and jumbled. I frantically palmed through, tossing them out into the hall. More shots came through the door, slashing through the holos and crackling against the walls behind.

Ah! There it was, still registering that last call we'd made from the *Majera*. I tapped to create a new message and picked out the letters: *"Pinned down. Deck…"* I looked around for some kind of sign to see which deck we were on. There was a big "4" emblazoned on the lift we'd gotten out of. That could be the deck or just the lift number. Oh well. *"Deck Four. Main accessway. Amidships battery under rebel guard. Trapped with Fareedh."* I paused again, then finally settled on simply ending with *"Help!"*

Another shot sizzled through the scattered displays. I gathered them up and reduced them. Maybe they were causing the shooters to burn through their energy, but I wanted to attract as little attention as possible. They might have grenades.

I looked up at Peter and put a finger to my lips. He nodded, a fearful shudder convulsing him for a moment. Marta looked a question at me. I showed her the *sayar* and she nodded. She looked over Fareedh while I stared at the message display, willing Iskender to answer.

Suddenly, there it was. *Stay put. Isra heading your way from bow.*

Isra. I tried to remember. Oh, the one Iskender had put in charge of the security detail. Perfect. When the team showed up, we could probably get back to the lift in the confusion. I tapped Marta on the hip, and she bent down to look at the message.

I whispered in her ear, "How's Fareedh?"

Her worried face said everything.

As if in punctuation, another tremor went through the deck. This one felt odd, like the gravity controls had flickered. Had they been hit? Sabotaged? If they went out while *Faucon* was doing high gee maneuvers, we'd all be plastered against the wall. I looked over at Peter. He nodded. He'd felt it, too.

Another message appeared on Fareedh's *sayar*: *Engine hit. Can't outrun. Batteries not responding. Not enough firepower.*

Marta whispered over my shoulder. "The rebels must have a hold of the batteries."

I swallowed. *What you want us to do about it?* I sent to Iskender.

A moment later, his response came, an echo of mine: *Help!*

"We've got to do something," Marta hissed.

"Like *what?*"

Marta looked at me, her round face set in grim determination. She leaned forward to whisper in my ear. "Okay. I think it's about twenty meters to where those shots came from. Stunners won't shoot that far. We've got to get closer."

I gripped her shoulders and whispered in her ear, "Are you loonie? You want to assault trained spacers under cover? We'll be cut down in seconds. They're playing for keeps."

"I've got an idea," she said. "A couple of them."

My inner ear quivered as another pulse ran through the ship. Everything seemed to slant a little bit, then returned to normal. The *Faucon* had probably tried to dodge something with a sideways thrust. I shivered. We shouldn't have felt it at all. The gravitics were surely going out.

"What's your plan?"

She looked down at one of the beamers at her hip, then back at me. Her fingers curled, then burst open. "Boom," she mouthed.

I could feel my forehead furrowing. I didn't even know you could do that with a beamer. Rigging one to blow up seemed like a job for Peter, and he might as well have been a thousand kilometers away.

But we didn't need Peter. Marta calmly pulled a small all-tool from her hip bag and went to work, disassembling her beamer. I felt silly. If Marta could maintain *Majera's* air system, she was as much an engineer as Peter. For a moment, the fear and worry was replaced by other feelings I wasn't even sure how to describe. I watched her work with newfound appreciation. It was hard to believe that this grime-faced woman peering into the guts of a deadly pistol was the flighty girl who'd dragged me from store to store for prom dresses just three years ago.

I commed to Iskender: "*Aye aye,*" and stuck the *sayar* back on Fareedh's belt.

Marta's fixes didn't take long. As she slapped the outer case back on her beamer, an explosive roar sounded from ahead. Shots followed in what seemed like an exchange of fire. Had Isra already arrived? Marta stood up, sticking the gimmicked beamer to her belt. Then she looked pointedly at me, then at Fareedh, and took his shoulders. I looked worriedly at her for confirmation. She nodded firmly. Moving Fareedh seemed like a bad idea to me, but what else could I do but trust her?

I took Fareedh's feet, and we hefted him off the sled as gently as we could, laying him on the deck as close to the wall as possible. He didn't even stir, his eyes closed the entire time.

Marta took her *sayar*, called up several displays, and flung them across the hall in front of the lip Peter was hiding behind–doing on purpose what I had done before on accident. Almost immediately, shots tore through the displays, sending sparks flying. Peter backed against his wall, eyes wide. Then Marta grabbed the floating bed, stood it on end, and charged through the open blast door using the sled like a Roman shield.

Chapter 17

I sprang to my feet, then cringed back as blasts ricocheted off her makeshift shield, sending sparks every which way. She plucked the gimmicked beamer from her belt and hurled it from behind the sled. It sailed across the wide corridor, clattered onto the deck, then flashed. A wave of heat and compressed air nearly knocked her off her feet.

"Go!" Marta shrieked, drawing her other beamer and charging forward. Without even being aware of what I was doing, I raced after her, a stunner in each hand. The makeshift bomb had left hardly a trace except for a brown discoloration on the walls, ceiling, and deck, but a charred figure lay sprawled on the deck on the right side near an open portal. That must have been where they'd sniped at us from.

I caught a flicker of motion in the portal: an armored spacer appeared, leveling a pistol at Marta.

"Marta, look out!" I screamed. Behind her shield, she couldn't have seen him. There was a flash of flame and the crash of an impact. The sled flew from Marta's grip and she spun half around, her back now to the shooter.

I ran headlong toward the rebel, pressing the studs on both stunners. The tingling in my ears told me they were firing, but the spacer remained upright, completely unfazed. With casual ease, the mutineer turned their gun on me. I didn't stop, heading straight into the maw of the mutineer's gun, my thumbs throbbing with the pressure on their triggers. If I could just get close enough…

The spacer's cannon flared. It seemed I could see the bullet speed toward me. I knew it had to be my imagination. What projectile went that slowly? I dove for the deck, still firing the stunners, my ears now throbbing with the beams.

I crashed to the floor, skidding forward on my chest, arms stretched in front of me. My chin banged against the hard deck, casting stars in front of my eyes. Then a scorching heat struck me from above. I instinctively covered my head and flinched.

Stupid! I was an open target. I opened my eyes again in a panic, expecting the final shot. It came.

But not for me. The spacer suddenly shrieked, then fell forward nervelessly. Their pistol skittered loudly over the deck.

Dizzily, I saw figures at the far end of the hall. "Ho!" the closest one shouted, maybe 30 meters down the hall from us. "Kitra?" It was the voice I'd heard on the bridge when Iskender had dispatched the security team.

"Isra?" I called back, my voice hoarse.

She was a short woman, dark hair in a ponytail, wearing an officer's tunic and an ensign's stripe. With practiced precision, she led three other spacers in coveralls toward us, their guns pointed at the vacant portal that had been the sniper's nest. One trotted to the portal's jamb, unclipped an orb from their belt, and tossed it inside. A warbling sound, like the vibration of a badly tuned grav motor, set my teeth on edge. Once it stopped, the thrower sprinted inside the portal. A moment later the same spacer emerged.

"All clear. Three knocked out."

Isra nodded curtly, reaching for the *sayar* at her hip.

"Kitra, are you alright?" Marta asked, stumbling toward me. I groaned a yes in reply and got to my knees. That was as far as I got before my wobbly legs rebelled. I stayed in a crouch, blinked and looked behind us. The ceiling was a smoldering ruin. That last shot the mutineer had fired, the one I had watched head toward me, must have been some kind of rocket grenade. I started to shake. If it had hit me or Marta, that would have been it.

Marta hoisted me up, one arm supporting me around my waist.

A tremendous shudder rippled through the ship. Something ran over my insides from toe to head and back again with a rolling pin. Marta let go of me to put her palms to her ears and whined softly. There was still weight tugging at my boots, but it was now at something like half a gee, and weird forces clutched gently at my limbs.

"That's it for the gravitics," Peter gasped. "No high-gee maneuvering now. We're dead ducks."

"*Isra,*" the ensign's *sayar* squawked. *"We're on emergency power. We've got to have the main batteries online to return fire."*

"Main battery secure, skipper," she said coolly, her sharp-featured face an impassive mask. "Ready for a fire control team."

"No time. Get in there and plot a general solution."

There was the barest of pauses. "Yes sir. Going in now."

She looked at us appraisingly. "Any of you qualified on Type 4 weapons consoles?"

Marta and I looked at each other wide-eyed, then both shook our heads at the ensign.

"I can give it a try," I heard Peter say with a grunt. "But we've got to get our friend to sick bay."

I spun on wobbly legs to see him, the low gravity doing weird things to my balance. He had joined us, charred sled in tow. Fareedh once again lay unconscious on it. "Come with me," the ensign said curtly, grabbing Peter's bicep and half-hauling him through the door. That left me and Marta with the floating sled.

"We don't know how to get to…" I protested, but they were already inside. There was nothing to do but follow them.

The battery's fire control chamber was a big room with lots of panels and displays. A huge shaft ran straight into the middle of it. It looked more like some kind of laboratory than anything else, though I hadn't really known what to expect. Isra was already at one of the stations. She said laconically without looking at us, "We'll get your friend to sick bay, but if we don't get this shot off, it won't matter anyway." Isra began manipulating her display. A now-familiar schematic popped up: Hyvilma surrounded by the transponder codes of ships. There was a new contact now, marked in red with the word *Hostile.*

"Solly," the ensign barked. "You've got a ship's *sayar* rating. Get us a firing solution."

A lean, mustached man in a coverall called out an "Aye, supe," and began fiddling at one of the stations.

"You, new guy," Isra said in the same tone. "See if those rebs left us any charge in the capacitors. If they drained them, we're sunk."

I looked at Peter. He hesitated, looking from station to station before deciding on one he liked and taking up position.

"What do *we* do?" Marta asked.

"Sit tight," Isra answered. "One way or another, this'll be over in a minute."

I stole a look at Fareedh. His face was ashen, but there was still some color in it. Marta brushed his hair aside and felt for a pulse, watching his chest rise and fall. She secured the straps that kept him on the sled and nodded slightly.

Peter called out, "Full charge! All channels open. No obstructions to firing."

"Very well," Isra said calmly. "Solly, that solution?"

"Yes, supe. Working on it. Target is not evading."

"Supe!" one of the others shouted. "Picking up an energy signature. The hostile's preparing to fire again."

I felt Marta's hand take mine. I gripped it hard. I'd never felt so helpless.

"Solly?"

"Almost. 80% accuracy window. 85%. 90%."

The one at the sensor panel shouted, "Discharge signature, supe!"

"Give it to me now, Solly."

"Transferring. It's only 93%, supe…"

"Good enough!" Isra shouted, jabbing two fingers at the red square floating in her display.

Everything happened at once. A roar came from overhead, like a clap of thunder, and the entire room rocked as if at sea. I clung to Marta like a buoy. Alarms clanged through the room, the zero-gee warning and sirens I didn't recognize. Half the displays winked out of existence.

The room lurched again. Marta and I flew sideways, headed straight for a bulkhead. She let go, and agile as a gymnast, spread eagled herself in front of me to cushion the blow. I crashed into her, causing Marta to oof audibly. Fareedh's bed came careening toward her. She reached for it, the muscles of her arms corded as she kept Fareedh from slamming into the wall. Then we all rebounded, drifting slowly back the way we came.

An unfamiliar voice came over the shipwides. "*Main batteries depleted. Gravitics off-line. Main engine circuits overloaded. Powerplant on standby,*" it called in a rush.

This was it, then. We'd been hit. Our power was gone. If we hadn't gotten our shot off, their next shot would surely obliterate us.

But Solly whooped happily. "Dead hit, supe!"

"Damage assessment," Isra called back.

"Get a load of this!" he cried, throwing the display to fill the center of the room.

A dark shadow floated through the unwinking starfield. A moment later, the shadow took on neon outlines, and an updating graph appeared next to it. The curve had gone from the top of the chart to somewhere near the bottom, where it quivered slightly.

"We broke its back. Power utilization curve is down to minimum."

Peter rubbed his halo of blond hair, clutching a handle on his station with the other hand. "We must have hit the transformers."

"Skipper," Isra commed, "Hostile has been neutralized."

"Can confirm. Good shot."

We weren't going to die! We'd done it!

Still floating, I buried my face in Marta's chest. I didn't know whether to cheer or sob. When I looked up, a quavering grin was on her face. Marta, her blotched cheeks wet with tears, her singed curls billowing crazily, was the most beautiful sight I'd ever seen. I…

I pulled her close and kissed her.

A shock went through me as my lips touched hers. She responded without hesitation, hungrily. Her arms slid around my waist, and I did likewise with her. It was like coming home. Tears welled behind my eyelids. Why did we have to nearly die to do this again? Why had we ever stopped?

There was a tugging at my boots, the grav systems coming online again, and we drifted lazily to the floor. Our feet touched deck, and I gently broke the kiss. Her eyes shone, gazing down at mine.

"Uh," Peter began. We both looked at him, our arms still around each other. "We need to get Fareedh to the sick bay." He looked meaningfully at him, lying in the sled oblivious to the world.

Isra joined us with an odd, skipping gait in the still-low gravity. "I'll take you. Solly, wait here for the ordnance team to relieve you. Call out additional sightings if there are any. Not that we'll have the juice to shoot back at this point."

Chapter 18

In sharp contrast to when we first infiltrated the *Faucon*, the corridors to sick bay were anything but empty. Damage control teams trooped past us in vacuum suits, lugging repair kits. Injured spacers on sleds, some pulled by other injured spacers, jogged alongside us. It was like this part of the ship had suddenly become the center of activity.

When we got to sick bay, it was obvious why.

The *Faucon's* main sick bay was way bigger than the one we'd left Sirena and Pinky in. Two dozen beds, each with their own diagnostic panel, ran in neat rows. If there had been any privacy partitions, they'd all been removed. They needed the space. As it was, there were patients that hadn't been taken off of their sleds for lack of beds. The place was frantic with activity, medics in white disposable tunics flitting from bed to bed. It was obvious there weren't enough of them. In a single glance, I took in more burns and blood than I ever wanted to see in a lifetime.

"There's no way Fareedh's going to get the help he needs," Peter exclaimed upon entering. "Look at this place."

"Maybe we should try to find the other sick bay," I said.

Marta was still holding my hand. She squeezed it and said, "No, I can help here. And they can use a real doctor, too. Let's see if Sirena can't bring Pinky."

I reached for my *sayar*, then remembered again that I'd left it on the flag bridge.

"I've got it," Peter said, taking his. I let Marta's hand go, now somehow self-conscious.

Sirena's face appeared above Peter's device. "Yes, darling, what is it?"

"Are you swamped?" Peter asked.

"Business has, how you say, picked up in the last fifteen minutes, yes. But just a few people, mostly minor wounds. Where are you?"

"Main sick bay. Look."

He held up his *sayar*. Sirena's bronze face blanched.

"Dios mío," she breathed.

"Yeah. At least one doctor's dead. Maybe all of them, for all I know. Fareedh needs help."

Marta cut in, "They all need help."

Sirena nodded. "Pinky is stable, and the other patients are ambulatory." She looked away, addressing someone off-display. "You, *sargento*, we are closing up shop. Can you take me to the main sick bay? *Bueno*." She looked back at Peter. "We will be there as fast as we can." Her image winked out.

Marta gave Peter's shoulder a squeeze. "You watch Fareedh. I'm going to see what I can do."

"You're an angel, my love," he said gravely, and kissed her. She smiled at that, then made off for the sterilizing station. I blew out a breath I didn't realize I was holding. Finally, things looked like they were about to be under control.

"We really don't deserve her," I heard Peter say, so low I almost couldn't make it out over the noise of the infirmary.

"We?" I asked.

He shrugged, then made a show of looking down and brushing Fareedh's hair out of his face. "Did I say 'we'?"

My cheeks burned. "You did."

Peter looked up at me, his smile lopsided. "Well, I mean, there's no question *you* do. You saved us all today, too."

"Don't be silly. We couldn't have made it here without you."

"I guess." He seemed unconvinced. "Anyway, it's nice to see you two together again."

I blinked. "What?! We're not…that was just…oh come *on*, Peter!"

A look I couldn't read came over his angular face. Was it disbelief? Anger? It was gone almost as soon as it had appeared. He cleared his throat. "My mistake then."

I looked away. My eyes fell on Marta, already putting on a white smock. *Together*? Me and Marta? No, that just wasn't possible. For every reason. And for goodness' sake, was this even time to worry about such things?

Apparently it was. A strange pang tugged at my chest. A familiar pang, I realized. How long had it been going on? Since Hyvilma? Since Jaiyk? I cast back through my memories, and one came to the fore, like the shard of a kaleidoscope. When I first told them all about the ship, before it even had a name, at Erkki's coffee house. Marta coming in with Peter and tousling his hair. I'd wrinkled my nose in distaste and told myself they really looked better together than she and I had.

I had no right to be jealous, and I certainly had no right to be a girlfriend stealer. Especially Marta. I'd broken up with her, after all, and for what seemed like the right reasons. As for couples, nothing seemed as natural as Marta and Peter, Peter and Marta.

But that kiss. I still felt echoes of it on my lips.

Sirena and Pinky arrived just a few minutes later. Somehow, I'd expected more of a reaction–the dazzling princess in her silver egg leading a bruised-looking lump on a floating stretcher. Scarcely anyone noticed. One grim-faced medic looked up at the newcomers, then at me.

"Is that the doc?" the stocky man asked.

I nodded, getting up from my chair. The deck seemed to wobble, then straighten out. I put a hand to my forehead. I hadn't realized how tired I was. How could Marta keep running around after all we'd been through?

Peter put a steadying hand around my arm and walked me to the entrance. I got my first look at Pinky since we'd left him in the larboard sick bay. He looked bad, a deflated ball with translucent liquid packs taped to it. His skin, instead of its usual soft rubbery look, seemed coarse and dry. I looked to Sirena, tried to speak, and failed.

A sound like a muted tug-horn came from Pinky, and his body quivered. As I watched, the fluid in the taped bags gurgled, and his cracked skin smoothed over some.

"Why so glum, chum?" he said in a hoarse whisper. "The party's just started. After all, I'm here."

I barked a laugh wrapped in tears and threw my arms around him. His bags crinkled, and I could feel his labored breathing against my cheek, hot and scented like cardamom.

"It's good to see you too, Kitra. It was kinda lonely without you." His voice was quiet, but it sounded more like himself.

I sniffled. "I'm not going anywhere without you again."

"Okay."

I felt a hand on my shoulder. Sirena's, I saw, looking up.

"I'm going to see what I can do here," she said. "You take care of my patient." With a wink, she glided into the room.

Pinky quivered underneath me. "Hey, Peter. Did you know there's grease all over your face?"

Peter wiped a paw across his cheek and made a face at what got left on his hand. "Wha…oh, gross. Why didn't anyone tell me?"

"Shame," Pinky said weakly. "I was about to be flattered. I thought I'd started a color-changing trend."

"Who'd want to look like you, anyhow?" Peter retorted.

"You're just jealous. I look amazing," Pinky wheezed. "In all seriousness, it is nice to see you, too. It's good to be…here." He quivered again, then shivered, like he did when he was about to change shape.

"Take it easy, pal," Peter said. "You don't have to do a thing."

Pinky settled for growing a little arm, stubby fingers emerging at its tip. They found my hand and clung.

"Hey, Kitra, where's Fareedh?" he asked. "I've got a good joke for him."

"He's here, too. Don't worry." The words came out thin.

"Show me," he insisted.

I looked up at Peter. He nodded briefly and said, "Sure thing, buddy," reaching for the bed's tow handle.

Fareedh was hooked up to something permanent, fluids running into his arm. He didn't look any better, but the wavering lines and occasionally changing numbers on his floating display at least gave reassurance that he was still with us. He didn't stir when Peter clinked Pinky's bed lengthwise to his.

"He looks almost as good as me," Pinky said, reaching out with his pseudopod. "What happened?"

"Someone shot him." I heard Peter grinding his teeth.

"That wasn't very nice." Rubber pseudo-fingers glided millimeters over Fareedh's chest, where Doctor Marku had stretched the temporary bandage. I winced, remembering Marku's death, the blast of fire and the crumple of a corpse.

Pinky was saying, "He smells like blood."

"Not enough," Peter mumbled. "He doesn't have enough."

Pinky touched Fareedh's face. "I wish I could give him some of mine."

"I don't think that would be good for either of you, darling," Sirena called from behind us. I stepped aside so she could float to her patients. She frowned over Fareedh's vital signs a moment, then cracked her knuckles. Despite everything, I found myself chuckling; it seemed a very unprincessy thing to do.

She ran her hands over Fareedh's bandage. I saw that she'd sprayed on gloves. She must be planning to do some kind of surgery. As if reading my thoughts, she said, "Yes, this won't do. I'm going to need to close this more permanently." Her dark eyes caught mine. "If you're squeamish, you'll want to look away. In fact, for cleanliness, you'll want to step back a pace."

"Let's give the doctor some room," Peter said. "We're just in the way here."

But there wasn't really space in the crowded sick bay, either. Finally, we ended up back in the corridor, me, Peter, and Pinky.

I sat on the deck with my back against the wall, arms folded. I didn't have anything left to say. It kind of felt like I never would again. There was a foggy ringing in the back of my head, and nothing else. My eyelids closed. I tried to think about Fareedh, or Pinky, or the *Faucon*, but my mind wouldn't engage. It had been run to the limit, and now it just wanted to hibernate.

"You hungry?" I heard Peter grunt. I opened my eyes, and he was offering me a skinny maroon brick. With surprise, I realized I was famished. I accepted the bar gratefully and pinched the end. The glistening wrapper atomized, and I took a brown bite. Savory sweetness splashed on my tongue. I recognized it as one of Peter's bulk-up protein-and-electrolyte rations, good for thirst and hunger. It was gone in a few snapped bites, and he reached for his pouch to get another.

I waved it away. "I don't know how you eat those all the time. They stop me up."

Pinky raised a finger, "Speaking of which, did I ever tell you about the time…"

"Not now, Pinky!" Peter and I said in unison.

His blue-tinted skin flickered mauve for a moment. Then he added, "I was just going to tell you about the first time I saw Fareedh."

"Didn't you meet him with us at *Le Frontiére*?" Peter asked.

Pinky quivered. "There was a time before that."

I leaned forward and looked up into his eyespots.

"What happened?"

He shifted on his sled, maybe getting more comfortable, and gestured with his pseudopod.

"So there I was, on a tour of the Institute, senior year in high school. Me and about a half dozen other classmates." Pinky's voice was stronger, and there was a resonant quality to his delivery. It made me hopeful.

"Of course, being an adventurous soul, I contrived to explore the campus on my own, and I quickly shed my companions."

Peter snorted. "You mean you got lost."

Pinky waggled a finger. "I *never* get lost. I knew exactly where I was. I just didn't know where *they* were. Anyway, I was taking in the sights. You know the big fountain in the hedge sculpture garden?"

We both nodded. It was in the engineering quad.

"Well, I'd gotten kind of bored and thirsty, and no one else was around, so I just sort of extended a trunk to take a drink."

"Eww," I said. "In the *fountain*? You know what people toss in that, right?"

"You know I'm not picky. Anyway, that's when I heard a bunch of folks coming up the walk, chattering away. I don't know why, but I just sort of froze. And then I thought, if I didn't want anyone to see me, I needed a disguise. So I made myself into a bush."

I smiled. I could totally see that. He'd taken on a similar camouflage on Purité, dappled green and bumpy. Worked pretty well, too. At least until he started moving.

"Along comes this tall fellow with flyaway hair, clearly the center of attention of an adoring throng, and half a head taller at that. At first, it looked like he was going to pass right by me. Then he stopped mid-sentence, turned to one of his friends, and asked, 'Was this hedge always here?'"

I giggled. Pinky went on, "So he's staring right at me, big brown eyespots getting closer and closer, until he's like half a meter away. I started to itch all over from the scrutiny. Finally…"

"Yeah?" Peter prompted.

"I sneezed."

"You don't sneeze," I objected.

"I did this time! Like a pneumatic subway. Fareedh must have flown back half a decameter. By the time he'd gotten up, I'd gotten myself pink again and normal-shaped. Well, people-normal, anyway. I put a hand on my hip and the other in a salute and said the first thing that came to mind: 'Hello! You are happy to meet me!'"

Peter brayed a high-pitched laugh, and I joined in.

"Fareedh had no idea what to make of me. I don't know if he thought I was kidding or that was the best French I could manage. Either way, it was pretty clear he'd never seen one of my kind before. I stuck out a hand, you know, to shake, and he looked at it like it might bite. Which invited another temptation…"

I laughed, "Pinky, you didn't."

"I didn't bite him! Not really. Just, when he put out his hand, I sort of…engulfed it." He paused for effect. "It's the only time I've heard Fareedh's upper register."

Peter was making choking sounds, wiping tears from his eyes. Finally, he managed, "So that's why Fareedh gave you the stink-eye that first time. I wondered why he was so jumpy around you."

"Why didn't he ever tell me?" I asked.

Pinky said, "I think he didn't want to hurt your feelings. When he saw we were best friends, I guess he decided to give me another shot." His tone got gentler. "I'm glad he did."

"You guys are two of a kind," Peter said. "Sometimes too much of a kind."

"You're just jealous of our keen…" Pinky stumbled on the last word, lapsing into a sort of cough.

"You all right, buddy?" Peter was concerned all at once.

"I…I may have put…too much of me…into…" His pseudopod melted into his body, and his whole bulk began to ripple ominously.

Chapter 19

"No, no, no, no, no," I babbled. "Pinky!"

There was no answer.

I bruised my hand against the door plate getting the portal open and hauled Pinky's bed back inside. Sirena was nowhere to be found in all the chaos. Finally, I spotted a glint off the back of her chair and a flash of red hair.

"Sirena! Pinky's in trouble," I hollered.

She didn't seem to hear me. I turned to Peter and pleaded, "Watch him, please."

He gave me a jerky nod and looked down at Pinky, now visibly deflated again.

There was an endless blockade of beds and people between me and Sirena. More wounded must have come in through other doors. When I got to Sirena's side, she was intently at work on a woman with a wicked burn that ran from neck to shoulder. I licked my lips, waiting impatiently while she sprayed foam over the blackened wound.

Without looking up, Sirena asked gently, "What is it?"

"Pinky," I blurted. "He's had a relapse."

She nodded. "I will be there in a moment."

A touch on my shoulder caused me to jerk and whip around. Peter had brought Pinky with him. I don't know how he'd gotten that bed through the crowded room. By brute force, I guess.

"Okay," I heard Sirena say. "Let's see what we have."

My hands balled into fists while she pored over Pinky's display. She checked the bags taped to Pinky's skin, then shook her head slightly. "We're not out of fluid. As I said before, it's simply not sufficient to stabilize him. We need actual alien plasma."

"Maybe they've got…Pinky blood in the stores," I said breathlessly.

Sirena shook her head again. "According to the reading I've done, transfusions must be done directly with another being of his kind. It doesn't store."

Peter ran a hand through his hair. "Why would they have any, anyway? It's not like Pinky's got cousins serving on board."

A surge of renewed panic ran through me. "Then we have to get him down to Hyvilma. Maybe there's one of his kind down there."

"We didn't see any last time we were there," Peter said, "and even so, it'd take you at least an hour just to land. We don't have the ship."

I stared at Pinky. He wasn't even recognizable anymore. Just a blue, rumpled husk. I couldn't just watch him die. My thoughts spun. I could get a ship's boat and race it down to the planet, drop it right in the lot of the hospital if I had to. Except, what if *Faucon's* boats had been broken in the battle? And how would I know how to fly them anyway? And Peter was right; there probably *weren't* any of his kind on Hyvilma anyway. Lord, if only Pinky *did* have a cousin on board the *Faucon*.

I looked up, unseeing, and blinked.

What was it that had happened when we first boarded the cruiser? One of Iskender's team had stopped short and was sure the ship's comms officer was one of us. Except no one could have confused us for crew, certainly not Fareedh with his rainbow outfit. But that's who they'd been looking at. Him and Pinky.

I took in a deep breath. "Does anyone know where I can find L'éclair?" I bellowed.

Peter looked at me as if I'd lost my mind. My eyes swept the room. Now that attention was on me, I shouted the same line again.

One man, arm trussed up in a sling, looked up from his bed. "I thought *he* was L'éclair." He pointed with his free hand.

"No, this is Pinky. He's my friend." I didn't have to shout anymore. The only sounds were our words and the low hum and ping of medical machinery.

"I coulda sworn…okay. I left him on Deck Six. Uh, ship's *sayar* control."

I fumbled for my *sayar*, remembered again I didn't have it, real ized it didn't matter because it wasn't like I could patch into shipwide comms with it. "Can you call him?" I shot back.

He blinked half-focused eyes, then fumbled at his belt. He winced as he got his *sayar* out, his sling barking against the edge of the bed. But he made the comm, if a bit haltingly. There was a back and forth, too quiet to make out over the slowly recovering background of conversation. At last, he looked up at me. "He's on his way." The spacer settled back onto his bed and covered his eyes as if the effort had exhausted him.

There was a medic behind me, long hair in a bun under a turban. I joggled his elbow. "How long will it take to get here from Deck Six?" I asked.

"Three minutes, tops."

"Sirena, will he make it?" My voice was pleading.

The Atlántidan doctor looked at Pinky's vitals gravely before answering. "I don't know," she said quietly.

I blinked once, then again, but I still couldn't see. I reached for Pinky's hand, but it was gone, absorbed into him again. All I could do was put my palms flat against his skin. It was cool to the touch. Panicked, I read his diagnostic. The squiggles had dropped to zero.

"Don't go, Pinky!" I screamed, flinging my arms around him. I whimpered again, "Don't."

The flesh against my cheek jerked, and there was the briefest of exhalations. For a moment, there was a whiff of…coffee?

Behind me, I heard Peter gasp. "He's rallying!"

I looked up. I couldn't read any of the labels of Pinky's diagnostic through the tears, but the squiggles had risen. I hugged my friend again, crying.

The smell of coffee became stronger. Specifically, the kind of coffee bean I'd brought with us from Vatan to make the traditional Turkish brew. It was definitely coming from Pinky, strengthening with each of his exhalations, cold against my tears. He had generated scents before, usually for comedic effect, but never so specifically before.

He was communicating, I realized. Too weak to talk, he was telling me he was still there the only way he could.

"I hear you, Pinky," I said with a sniffle. "Hang on. We're all here."

Another exhalation, this time like a combination of sulfur and barbecue sauce. My lips curled, and I felt a chill roll up my spine. Was it some kind of death gasp? Then I recognized the odor and breathed a sigh of relief. Unpleasant, it certainly was, but also unmistakable. Not something to worry about.

I sobbed a little laugh. "Yes. Peter's here, too. That was a long time ago, though. Don't hold it against him."

Pinky's flank quivered slightly. Maybe the closest to a chuckle he could manage.

"What did I do?" Peter asked.

"Don't worry about it." I gave Pinky a pat. "He just said he loves you, too."

"Oh…" he said.

I lay against Pinky for what felt like ages. As long as those laborious breaths continued, I knew he was still with us. As long as I clung to him, I was sure he couldn't leave.

Someone shook my shoulder. Without moving my arms from around Pinky, I looked up.

It might have been Pinky's twin. Except for the skin having a more yellowish tinge, the being before me was virtually identical: two eye-spots looked down at me from just above my eye level. They lay side by side in a round hump of a head. The rest of the alien was in what I called "standard Pinky configuration" — three arms and two legs. Unlike Pinky, he wore clothes. They were the same black and gold of the officers on the *Faucon*, but the uniform was form-fitting and probably malleable, like Pinky's suit. It was no wonder the crew of the cruiser had mistaken Pinky for one of their own. Lieutenant's stripes girdled all three of its wrists, and there were little lightning bolt symbols at the rim of the neck.

I cleared my throat. "L'éclair, I presume?"

"The same," he answered, in a round, deep holostar's voice. "Your friend is in a bad way."

I swallowed the lump in my throat. "Yeah. Can you help? Sirena… the doctor…says he needs a transfusion."

L'éclair eyed me expressionlessly a moment, then looked at Pinky. "Do you mean take some of me and put it in him?"

Sirena spoke up, "Just fluid, to stabilize him. His system is out of balance."

The communications officer flushed beige. "There's no such thing as just fluid in me. It's *me*."

Sirena frowned. "Do you mean we cannot effect a donation?"

L'éclair shook his head in a very human expression. "That is not what I mean. It's just that, while the flesh is willing, the spirit is weak, if you take my meaning. I do not think it will do him good, at least, not the way you're contemplating."

Exasperated, I cried out, "Well, what can we do?"

He seemed to think about that. Meanwhile, Pinky shuddered, his breath rasping more loudly. At last, L'éclair looked at me again. "If I can help, I must. But, I can't do it here. It is a private thing. I will take him elsewhere."

"I can't leave him!" My answer was immediate and reflexive.

Again he was silent. His eyespots dropped, their gaze resting on my hands. Pinky's flesh had dimpled and fingertip growths seemed to cradle my fingers. I hadn't noticed when he'd done that.

L'éclair nodded. "I see that. Very well. Please come with me."

Chapter 20

The room was not much more than a big closet. Its door had been marked "Subsystem Control 4", and inside, there was a seat, a shelf, and a ship's *sayar* station. No one had been in there when we'd gone in. It was the closest private room to the sickbay.

The alien spacer looked at me fixedly. "His time is close. I am not a doctor, but I can tell. I may not be able to help him, and if I can, there may be…side effects. For both of us." His skin tinged toward vermillion. "I hope you don't have secrets you really don't want shared."

I found myself gripping two of his shoulders. "If you can save him, I don't care about anything else. Please."

Without preamble, L'éclair tugged at his collar. The skintight uniform came apart like the peel of a purple, quickly leaving him completely nude. He had the same soft, rubbery skin as Pinky—at least, when Pinky had been healthy. The alien spacer ran quivering hands over the flank of my sick friend. The movements seemed patterned, even ritualistic, like the Ocak healers who still treated patients in the heart of Vatan's capital. L'éclair's probing pseudo-fingers lengthened into tentacles, and Pinky's skin underneath began to mottle. No, not mottle, *bubble*.

With a lurch, L'éclair's hand-tendrils went into Pinky. I gasped, watching the alien officer's body slowly melt into formlessness, becoming a dumpy orange sphere with a single limb that arced seamlessly into Pinky's body. L'éclair shuddered, and the branch of flesh that joined him with Pinky tinted green.

A rushing sound, like wind rising through trees, chorused from their merged forms, becoming words. "We decay!" it said. "Everywhere is rot. We waste."

The linking tentacle contorted like a clogged fueling hose. The merged form cried out, "It hurts. We cannot. Please." I couldn't tell if it was Pinky crying in pain or L'éclair losing his nerve. Or both. A clash of sounds came from the joined pair, along with an indescribable scent, harsh and alien. Then, the bond of flesh thickened, the mass for it clearly coming from Pinky's end.

"We cannot go. They need us," the combined voice said.

Pinky crept off the bed, pouring onto the floor like a melting ball of wax. L'éclair recoiled, as if from flame. But the room was small, and there was nowhere for him to go. Now Pinky was completely on the floor, his entire body tinged a faint teal. The bed glistened with evil-looking goo.

The end that had been L'éclair cried plaintively, "Who are we?"

A voice, almost-human toned, replied, "We are. That is enough."

More than the tentacle connected them now. They were like two amoebas merging together. I fought back tears, fists balled. Would there even *be* a Pinky when this was done?

"We cannot see," whimpered some part of the merged being

"The we who are not we can see," it answered itself. Then in almost recognizably Pinky tones, it rasped, "Kitra. Make the circle."

The circle. I stared in confusion. Then I remembered: Pinky walking an orbit around the frozen sleepers on the *Émilie*. Pinky circling my house and then enfolding me in comforting arms after my mother had died. I crouched and put my arms around both of them, placing myself in the crease that showed they were still independent beings.

They rippled, the sickly teal fading to a neutral beige. "We are," the merged form chorused. "We are."

It was too warm. I was almost smothered by the quivering, sharp-smelling alien flesh. But their skin was smooth and dry, with none of the slime Pinky had left on the bed. Flashes of scent came first from one end of the connected pair, then the other. Lubricant oil. Pine. The wet salt of the *Lodos* blowing from the Denizli coast. And other, unclassifiable odors. They had stopped speaking, at least in French. Now it was a low gibbering that faded to and from a whisper. Perhaps this was their native language, or maybe it was like the purring of a cat. Before, they must have been speaking French for my benefit. I hugged them more tightly.

Over time, the feverish flesh cooled to a tolerable, familiar temperature. Where my nose had been pressed against alien hide, a depression had formed, allowing me to breathe comfortably. Through the closed door, I heard an announcement on the shipwide comms, too muffled to make out, except that it was probably Iskender speaking. The tones were strong and reassuring. Good news, I hoped.

I felt my head start to drift toward the ground. I gripped their hides to stay up, and my arms started to pull apart. They were separating, I realized. I bobbed back on my heels and let them go.

Pinky was almost pink! Not quite the ruddy healthiness I was used to, but the bluish tinge was definitely gone. A smile came to my lips, then froze as I looked over at L'éclair, now a separate entity again. He was a sort of limbless, lopsided figure eight, with the fatter end resting on the ground, and the two eyespots in the smaller end up top. His skin was the same color. In fact, looking from one to the other, it was impossible to tell them apart; Pinky had taken on the same shape. Both were looking fixedly at me.

"Hello," they chorused.

My smile faltered. "Hello."

"You are Kitra." Again, the voice came from both of them.

I swallowed. "That's right. You are…" I looked first at Pinky, then at L'éclair.

The response was a disjointed thing, sometimes together and sometimes apart, like one of those two-part spoken word songs that students recited at *Le Frontiére*:

"We are…

                      "We.   I.

            "What we were.   Am now.

"Two.

                                      "One.

                "The being that was.

                                  "Pinky.

"L'éclair."

The dry ship's air was harsh in my nostrils as I breathed in sharply. Had they merged in more than body? Were the two of them now some sort of weird combination? L'éclair had said there would be side effects, but this seemed a lot more than a side effect. My chest began to throb. If I'd essentially killed two beings instead of losing one...

"You sadden," they said, warmth growing in the tones.

I sniffed and nodded wordlessly.

"No need.

"All is well."

I watched, dry-mouthed, while the two aliens pulsed in silent communion. Finally, they began again.

"We should.   I will.

"We are.

"We are no longer.

"We.

"I.

"Yes, I.   Yes, I."

Their voices faded, and their forms seemed to pulse. As I watched, the one on the right shifted hue subtly, from peach toward pink. On the left, skin shaded toward the sallow end. The rightward one grew two little stumps to either side. As I watched they became arms. Their tips differentiated into hands with fingers.

Displaying the "OK" sign.

"It's me, Kitra!" Pinky said, his voice completely familiar, if a little weak.

I brushed hair and tears out of my eyes. My ponytail had gotten half undone. I looked at L'éclair. He, too, was returning to his old configuration. Once he had legs, he managed a bow.

"Lieutenant L'éclair, at your service," he said a little breathlessly. He swayed on his new legs, and I rushed to hold him upright.

He continued apologetically. "I'm afraid that took rather a lot from me." His eyespots meandered to face Pinky's. "But I am not sorry for what I received. I did not know that the bond between our kind and yours could be so strong. Almost a one-ness."

Pinky gestured, palm out. "We're best friends," he said, as if that explained everything.

I wiped tears away from my cheeks and from under my silly grin.

I guess it did.

The sick bay had calmed down a lot in the time we were away, maybe 30 minutes. Sirena and Marta's presence seemed to have turned the tide. Beds were now in neat rows. Patients had their wounds dressed and were either chatting with each other or sleeping. The medics were no longer rushing from injury to injury. One was even sitting in a chair against the back wall, rubbing his eyes.

L'éclair went in first, waving jauntily. "Hello, everyone! Miss me?"

A mixture of greetings and good-natured jeers was the general reply. One patient called out, "Look who's Mr. Cheerful all of a sudden."

No sooner had I gotten through the door, than Peter was rushing toward us, his face lit up like it was Hannukah. "You did it! Sweet infinity, you did it!" He goggled at Pinky unbelievingly. "It's a miracle, for sure. How're you feeling, pal?"

Pinky padded over silently and put a pseudopod out, resting his hand on Peter's arm. He made a show of tapping his stubby fingers against the skin and making "hmm" noises. At last, he said, "Apparently, I *feel* just fine."

Peter snorted with a roll of his eyes. "Yeah, you're just fine, alright."

"I am. Just a little tired. Thank you for asking, really." He extended his head to peer over Peter's shoulder. "How is Fareedh doing? Can I see him?"

"I don't know, *can* you?" Peter said, giving Pinky back some of his own before adding, "Seriously though, I think he'd be hurt if you didn't. He woke up about ten minutes ago, and he wouldn't go back to sleep until he knew you were okay."

Sure enough, when we got to him, Fareedh was already propped up on one elbow, the other arm reaching out despite the tubes running from it. Sirena chided him ineffectually. Pinky leaned forward and gave him a three-armed hug.

"Nice to see you again," Fareedh murmured dazedly. He was still pale as anything.

"Nice to be seeing, my friend."

Pinky flattened to the floor, leaving one of his pseudopods up in the grip of Fareedh, who at last gave in to Sirena's gentle pressure and lay down. The second his head hit the pillow, his eyes closed.

"How is he?" I asked Sirena.

"Just fine, darling. Patched up and full of borrowed blood. In two days, when his stomach is healed, we can start to fatten him up again."

Peter chuckled, "The stringbean can use it."

"What did I miss?" Pinky asked. "The last thing I remember clearly is passing out in the other sickbay, and then the fight on Deck Six."

I looked at him quizzically. "You were never on Deck Six," I said.

"Of course I wa..." Pinky flushed maroon. "Ah, perhaps you're right. In any event, what has happened?"

"I suppose you missed the announcement," Sirena said, relaxing back in her chair and folding her slim arms in her lap. "The *Zafer*, that's the ship that attacked us, surrendered. Shortly after that, the rebels on Hyvilma signaled that they were also giving up."

Marta had joined us. Looking up as she bent to embrace Pinky, she said, "It was wonderful. You should have heard the cheer. We're headed for the *Zafer* now to take care of the wounded." She got up and slid an arm around Peter's waist. I did my best to fight a blush and chided myself. Peter and Marta. Marta and Peter. A natural pair. Perfect together. Remember that.

"Here's hoping they don't have some trick up their sleeve," I heard Peter say.

Fareedh mumbled, "My brother'll take care'f 'nyone." Sirena shushed him, and Fareedh's face slumped sideways into his pillow.

Almost sympathetically, a wave of exhaustion hit me too. My vision blurred, and the deck seemed to heave beneath me.

"Do you think I can spare a few minutes to sit down?" I asked, my voice already a little fuzzy. "I didn't realize how tired I was."

Sirena waved toward one of the walls. There wasn't a free seat, but there was a stretch of space between two displays. "The crisis is over, Kitra. You've earned a rest."

Marta smiled sweetly, "We'll join you soon, don't worry."

"I'll come with you," Pinky said. He extended legs and walked with me, half supporting me, as we made our way to the clear stretch.

I made to sit down, but he beat me to it, filling the spot. I looked at him in confusion until he'd completed his transformation. Now he was a pink cushion maybe a meter and a half wide.

"Are you sure?" I asked.

"You guys carried me here. The least I can do is return the favor," he said.

I didn't argue. I curled up on him, the warmest, softest bed imaginable. In moments, I was asleep.

Chapter 21

Launch +70

The Window in Captain Sirocco's cabin filled an entire wall, looking straight down on the full purple globe of Hyvilma. For a dizzying moment, I was back in space again with nothing but a line connecting me to safety, even with the solid anchoring of a chair to tell me I was actually safe and shipboard. I turned my head with an effort to focus on the skipper of the *Faucon,* seated at the end of the long oval table.

Sirocco was not physically impressive—she was tiny, in fact—but she had an air of age. Little wrinkles creased the corners of her lips and eyes, and her hair was an iron gray. Either she had not bothered with any of the age-retarding treatments or she was *really* old. Her skin was almost as pale as Peter's, but with a completely different tone, as if it would normally be much darker, if she ever saw the sun. It was the pallor of a true spacer, the kind that doesn't bother with shore leave.

I expected her to have the reedy, arid voice of a crone. She didn't.

"I hear you did a lot out there," Sirocco said in a pleasant alto. Her French had the polished accent of the Core worlds. I wilted a little under the attention, glancing at Marta, Peter, and Sirena to my left, then Fareedh and Pinky to my right. Fareedh was in a white patient's tunic, loosely belted. Pinky wore nothing at all, as usual.

I licked my lips. "No more than a lot of people, including Fareedh's brother."

The grooves at the corners of the captain's mouth deepened as she smiled. "Yes. The zeal with which he exerted himself was a bit of a surprise."

"Not to me," Fareedh said firmly. He added, "Captain."

"No, I suppose not." Sirocco's smile flickered. "And others surprised me in disappointing ways. That's my failing. Well, worry not. *First* Lieutenant Konak will be adequately recognized," she said. "I've also put him in for the CDA." She caught my blank expression and added, "For exceptional conduct and special sacrifice."

A white-uniformed orderly walked in with a tea service, setting saucers and cups of gleaming silver and porcelain before us. He poured each of us a precisely measured portion, pausing only when he reached Pinky. We all looked up expectantly. Without missing a beat, the immaculately dressed batman took what I thought had been a milk tureen and filled Pinky's cup with something that shimmered with oily iridescence. Fareedh wrinkled his nose slightly and shifted away. Pinky, on the other hand, leaned forward and flushed an unmistakably pleased rose.

"You know how to treat your guests," he said warmly.

"It has been my honor to serve with your kind," the captain said simply. Sirocco dismissed the orderly with a curt nod, and he whisked away without a word. She then took her steaming cup and raised it in a toast. "To the saving of the *Faucon*, and perhaps the entire sector."

Peter winced as the hot tea hit his lips. I smiled and sipped without reservation. The brew was just this side of boiling, as was appropriate.

Captain Sirocco replaced the cup on its saucer and looked down into it. "Speaking of recognition, I have no power to award commendations to civilians. However, this latest set of circumstances has caused me to review the powers I do have with some scrutiny. I am authorized to award battlefield commissions." Her eyes flickered up and speared me.

I pointed at myself, eyes widening.

"Yes. This incident was a test, and the loyalty of many was found wanting. Yours was not." Her chuckle was almost a purr. "Not that I would expect less from the daughter of Betül Yilmaz."

"You knew my mother?"

"Only professionally. In any event, I think 'Lieutenant Yilmaz' has a nice ring to it. What do you think of that?"

I felt a glow that started in my chest and spread to my toes and fingertips. I hadn't expected a reward for what we'd done. Honestly, Pinky being alive and well was reward enough. But I'd grown up surrounded by people with lofty titles, the Empire's cream. I hadn't understood their world, not really. I was far too young. But the pomp and the dazzle had always impressed me, and I'd been proud my mother was a respected part of that world. A lieutenant's rank was a rung into it.

Acceptance caught in my throat. I looked over at Fareedh. He'd been shot and could easily have died because of my 'loyalty'. It was with even greater uncertainty that I looked to my left. Marta's expression was fixedly neutral, as was Peter's, though a faint pink flushed his temples. Sirena just watched me with an arched eyebrow.

I coughed. "Captain, it's a huge honor. I want to accept." I licked my lips. "But we didn't get *Majera* to become privateers." Sirocco's eyebrows shot up at that, and I kicked myself mentally. "What I mean is, we don't want to lose our independence. Besides," I looked again meaningfully at my friends, right, then left, "Everybody did their share. I just drove us here."

The captain snorted at that, taking another sip of tea. "I can tell you are the type who sells herself short. But it is true. I, no *we*, are indebted to all of you. It's just that, for political reasons, it would be difficult to justify awarding a commission to any of the others." Her eyes roved uneasily over Sirena, Peter, and Marta before returning to me. "Especially right now, when the situation is still in flux."

Marta's tone was knife-edged, "You mean we're not the right sort. Politically."

The captain shot back. "Don't be naive, Ms. Jarvinen. You've earned *my* undying gratitude." Her tone softened. "Those are not empty words. I mean it. I recognize all that you did. But I can only award something like this to a person whose credentials no one will question. None of you are a Yilmaz."

"Did not Commander Akar have an impeccable pedigree?" Sirena asked softly.

The captain's right hand was on the table. Her fingers curled. "Which only ties my hands further. After what happened, anything I do will be looked at under a quantum scanner. The fact is this: this is the reward I can give, and she is the one I can give it to. You are obviously a team, and it is my hope that the benefits attached to the commission can be shared by all."

I sensed an opportunity. I leaned forward in my seat, clearing my throat again. "Alright. Then, one officer…" I smiled cannily at Marta, then looked back at Sirocco and added, "…potentially…to another, can you tell us exactly what did happen? Is this a civil war?"

Sirocco hesitated, taking a third sip of tea. Then she nodded. "I can tell you what I know, which at the moment, is somewhat limited. Frankly, until a ship arrives from Sennet, we can't know how far this movement has spread or if similar incidents aren't happening elsewhere."

The captain leaned back and rubbed her eyes, suddenly looking very tired. "Three days ago, Akar and several strategically placed officers took over this ship. You know that much. The *Zafer*, the destroyer you so ably helped engage day-before-yesterday, had timed its arrival to a full day before the coup. It was almost entirely crewed by mutineers."

"I'm surprised they surrendered," Fareedh observed.

Sirocco nodded. "We were, too, but that last salvo took down everything, even their batteries. There are gradations of fanaticism, even among zealots. They could not destroy their ship, and they did not relish the idea of slowly suffocating in the cold."

I shivered automatically in sympathy. It must have been obvious, because both Marta and Fareedh briefly put comforting hands on mine.

"The *Zafer* has a Jump 6," Sirocco continued, "and it came out of Talvi. They had a full platoon of Marines aboard, which took over Hyvilma's city hall, the spaceport, and broadcast stations. The Hyvilman gendarmerie is not armed, of course, so they posed no resistance.

"From our preliminary interrogation of the mutineers and those on the *Zafer*, we suspect the operation involved more than these two ships, perhaps even including elements of the First Fleet based at Sennet. On the other hand, we've confirmed that there are no other ships in this system, at least ones that shouldn't be here. If more vessels were supposed to join this operation, they either never arrived, or they are operating elsewhere."

I glanced over at Pinky. Was the 'pirate' we'd run into actually one of Akar's rogues? I discarded the idea as quickly as it had arisen. The timing was wrong. And what would be the point? If the rebels had just wanted more ships, they'd have had much better pickings around Hyvilma.

The captain went on, "Still, even just the *Faucon* and the *Zafer* would have made a formidable fleet. Considerable resources would have had to be devoted to neutralizing it, and who knows what damage they might have done in the interim."

"And this was really all the doing of the Trans-Frontier People's Front?" Peter asked. He did not sound convinced.

Sirocco pursed her lips. "It's difficult to say, but if they're involved, it is probably only part of the story. Akar's a clever fellow. He's not talking, but I suspect he was upper echelon in the operation, and his politics aren't so specific. He and his comrades probably said whatever would be most appealing at the time to the recruits. There are always people willing to listen to a rabble rouser. He spent considerable time on the planet, too. There's no telling what he was doing during shore leave. We'll have to thoroughly stamp out whatever he started."

I frowned. Akar hadn't seemed like the mustache-twirling type. He'd said things that made sense, especially knowing what I'd learned about history from Peter and Marta. He'd seemed as genuinely worried about the *Faucon* remaining in Imperial hands as Sirocco was about the cruiser becoming a rebel ship. 'A bloody police club,' he'd called it. A thought came to me. The planet we'd had to avoid on our first trip out from Hyvilma. The charts had marked it as interdicted.

"Is that why the Navy's quarantined GM +910? To suppress a rebellion?" I asked.

The captain's eyes were hooded. After a moment, she replied, "There is a valid medical concern."

Marta was still on the original subject. "So you suspect the Hyvilmans of working with the rebellion?" she asked.

"We have not yet assessed the level of local involvement in the operation. We'll have to go down and find out," Sirocco said tersely.

"But you think the rebels had help, right?"

"It would be difficult to believe the commandos could have taken over the city alone."

Marta's tone grew angry. "You mean you want to believe that. It'd be easier to crack down on everyone if you had that as a pretext, suspecting everyone on the planet."

Peter gripped Marta's arm gently, whether in support or in restraint, I couldn't tell.

Sirocco replied, "That's why we have to have an investigation."

"No!" Marta shot back. "I mean, yes, investigate, but don't go in with your minds already made up."

Fareedh broke in. "Uh, these rebels meant business. I think we should do what we can to make sure they're taken care of." He looked down at his chest, as if seeing through the cloth to the bandage beneath. "They shot me, you know."

Marta's eyes flashed. "Yes, Fareedh, and they shot at *me*, too." Her fists balled on the table. "And I killed them. I killed *people*." Now she was trembling with barely restrained emotion. It leaked into her voice. "I want to know why I had to kill people. No, I know why I had to. They were threatening my friends." She swallowed. "But that's done. We need to take a step back and see why this all happened in the first place. Not make it worse."

The captain shook her head, eyes incredulous. "You can actually sympathize with these…these butchers? After all they did?"

Peter snorted. "Captain, it's not like we're gonna vote for the FPTF in the next elections, not if they're really behind this. All she's asking is that you take it easy."

"This is a matter that goes to the heart of Imperial security. Who knows how far this insurrection has spread? Speed and intensity are of the essence. How exactly are we supposed to 'take it easy'?"

I looked at Marta. She looked back at me expectantly. Oh great. What was I supposed to do? I could see Sirocco's point of view. In a lot of ways, it was mine. The Empire were the good guys. The people shooting at them, at *us*, were the bad guys. It was the government's job to fact-find and resolve grievances. It was the kind of thing my mother might have been sent in to resolve, to defuse the situation with a deft, diplomatic touch.

Except she wasn't here. Sirocco was. And the captain had an axe to grind. She was justified, maybe, but still biased.

"I have an idea," I said. Immediately, all eyes were on me. My fingers itched to rub together. I put my palm flat on the table instead. Really, I only had half of an idea.

"What if," I continued, "you had a neutral third party be part of the investigation?"

"Are you serious?" the captain asked.

I nodded. The plan was coming together in my head. "Yeah. Three people. You, an elected Hyvilman, like the mayor or something, and a neutral person. All investigations and decisions go through this commission. Then it's not a military operation, and maybe you'll get more buy-in from the locals. The neutral will keep anyone from going too far."

"And just who would you recommend be this 'neutral'?" Sirocco asked.

"Well, I was thinking Sirena."

"A *Midworlder*?" The captain exclaimed, then looked instantly regretful.

To her credit, the princess didn't bat an eyelash. "Is not Atlántida a loyal, long-established member of the Empire?" she asked. "In addition, we have been traditionally uninvolved in frontier politics."

I suppressed a smile. That wasn't strictly true anymore. After all, the whole reason Sirena was here was to find a trans-Rift planet for colonization. But I knew I could trust her anyway. She was a lot older than me, and certainly a better diplomat.

"My apologies, your highness," Sirocco said with honest sentiment. "That was uncalled for." She looked over at me, then at Marta. Taking a deep breath, she said, "I suppose there could be merit to a team effort. I don't know when back-up is going to arrive. We may be on our own for a long time. It's probably best not to alienate the world we're orbiting. But by God, we will find out what happened and hold the criminals responsible." She was glaring at me for that last bit, with a bit of defiance and maybe respect.

"Thanks for listening to me, captain," I said. Then shyly, I added, "Do you, uh, still want to make me a lieutenant?"

The captain blinked. Then her face creased in a smile, wrinkles deepening, and she rumbled with laughter. At the same time, I felt Marta's hand take mine again, and she grinned at me gratefully. A warm thrill filled my chest.

"You are a bold one, Kitra Yilmaz," I heard Sirocco saying. I cleared my throat and looked at the captain. Said she, "And you want no conditions. Stripes but no stipulations."

I managed a nod.

"Very well. How about a reserve commission? Service rendered, complete with an honorable discharge."

Pinky extended a finger. "But what if there's a war? Won't she get called up? Get sent to fight the Grilchies?"

Sirocco waved the concern way. "The action on the Grilchie frontier is strictly regular Navy. The Empire hasn't declared a formal war in more than a century."

Peter mumbled under his breath, "Unless this insurrection was the first shot of a civil war."

The captain replied, her tone almost matchingly low, "In that case, you've already picked a side."

Goosebumps chilled my bare arms. She was right, and if we wanted to keep having influence on what happened, some kind of title would be useful. Boy, were we in over our heads. But we'd been that way since we made our first blind Jump to Jaiyk. When we rescued the settlers from Gloire. When we took on a freaking Navy cruiser. Why stop now?

"I'll take it, captain."

We were a subdued bunch as we left the captain's quarters. My mind kept oscillating like an electron jumping from layer to layer. The revolt, the honor, Marta. I needed something concrete to think about. Something grounded.

"Guys," Pinky said, "I'm hungry."

I was almost grateful to realize I was famished. We'd been living on scrounged bites the last twenty-four hours. The most solid meal we'd had was self-heating rations in the sick bay. And that was…how long ago?

Fareedh made a show of grasping his stomach. "Me too."

Marta tsked. "You're not supposed to eat until tomorrow."

"Give me a break. Getting shot takes a lot out of you." Pinky turned salmon in amused appreciation.

"I could eat a vat of Maker goop," Peter said. "Well, there's gotta be a galley someplace."

I chuckled, squaring my shoulders. "Surely, they can do better for a newly christened lieutenant," I said. Even without stripes on my sleeves, I felt like a swashbuckler. *Lieutenant* Yilmaz. It went nicely with the *Captain* Yilmaz I got by right of being master of *Majera*. Of course, right now, I'd settle for *fed* Yilmaz. "Peter, call up on your *sayar* where the officers' wardroom is. We're going to eat in style."

Stylish it was. Compared to the wood-paneled coziness of the chiefs' mess, the officers' wardroom was extravagantly large. There was wood here, but light and finely veined. Two long tables extended the length of the compartment, draped in gold-fringed purple cloth, and set with what looked like real silver, glass, and porcelain. More importantly, the smell of spices and savory cooking was faint but fresh, and my stomach practically caved in on itself in anticipation.

There was nobody here, though. Maybe we were between meal shifts.

Not quite nobody. A short, dark spacer with wisps of straight black hair over a sweat-beaded head strode purposefully up to us. His uniform was cut officer-style, but it was charcoal gray with only a wide silver stripe at the cuff. I didn't recognize it.

"I'm sorry," he said in a tone that didn't sound sorry at all. "This room is for officers only." He eyed our civilian clothes with suspicion and distaste.

I was taken aback only for a moment. With bland assurance, I pulled out my *sayar* and called up the lieutenant's credentials the captain had just given me. I was even wearing the same clothes as in the holo since Sirocco had taken it not thirty minutes before.

"This is my party...chief," I guessed. "I'm Lieutenant Yilmaz. You may have heard of me as *Captain* Yilmaz." Pointing, I added, "That's Lieuten...*First* Lieutenant Konak's brother, and this is Her Highness Sirena Isabella de Atlántida Jáimez."

"The Seventh," Sirena added demurely.

"Right. The Seventh." I glared at the spacer. "Do you need her credentials too?"

The man's expression softened considerably, and I felt a little guilty for putting on airs. But boy was it fun.

"That won't be necessary," he said smoothly. "Of course I recognize your voice. Congratulations on your commission, Lieutenant. Dinner's not for another hour or so, but I'm sure I can whip you all up something." He ushered us to one of the tables, pulling out a chair to give Sirena easy access. "Do you have any dietary restrictions?" he asked. Then he looked at Pinky, adding, "I assume your tastes are similar to those of Lieutenant L'éclair?"

Pinky plopped himself at the end of the table. "More than ever," he said. "A zucchini and sauerkraut mash, if you please."

The spacer didn't even blink. I, on the other hand, looked at my friend like he'd gone loonie. Yech.

"Anything but pork," Fareedh said, taking his seat.

"Me too," I added. The others expressed that they needed no special attention.

When we had all sat down, the spacer actually bowed slightly, like a maître d', and said, "I'll be right back. If you need anything, just call for Mister Rakotoson."

I smiled over at Sirena after the spacer had departed. "Goodness. We need to travel with you more often! Talk about service."

She shook her head. "I think he was fawning over you, *Captain*."

Marta giggled. "I think you're right. My hero!"

"'Do you need *her* credentials, too?'" Peter mimicked. "Man. Nobody better mess with you."

I blushed. "Too much?"

"Just right," Peter said. "I like 'em tough." He grinned at me, then glanced over at Marta, who gave him a playful punch in the arm.

"I think," Pinky interjected, "that he was paying deference to me. After all, I look far more like a certain lieutenant brother than Fareedh looks like his." He swiveled his eyespots to Fareedh. "Are you quite certain you are related to Iskender? You look nothing alike."

"Well, we can't be sure who the mother was," he murmured jokingly.

I laughed at that, a short burst before I felt my smile flicker. "Well, anyway, I'm sorry for volunteering you, Sirena."

She made a dismissive gesture, her earrings tinkling softly. "The plan was always for me to depart at Hyvilma. I am grateful for the extra time we got together, even given the circumstances."

"Either way, I just wanted to say, I…we…we're going to…" Suddenly, my throat didn't want to work, and my eyes were stinging.

Sirena smiled gently. "Consider the point made. I shall miss you all, too." Her eyes softened. "Oh, Pinky, I shall especially miss you. But please do not look so sad." I turned and saw Pinky had turned a faint green.

"You know what that color means?" I asked, impressed. It was a shade he rarely turned.

"Of course." She reached across the table to put a hand on one of Pinky's rough paws. "I have learned a lot in the last few days." He looked up, and the green faded somewhat. Pinky clasped Sirena's small hands in two of his.

Sirena went on, "Don't worry, darling. We shall see each other again. Just some business to attend to first."

From behind the serving door, the sounds of clinking dishes and a hiss of steam suggested that the meal would be ready soon.

Marta asked, "Is this going to interfere with your plans? The commission duty, I mean." Her tone was light, but I saw that she had unconsciously touched fingertips to her earrings, the ones Sirena had given her for her birthday.

"I should think not," the princess replied. "I just need to send a message on the next ferry or mail boat bound for Punainen. It will have all the details about the new world and the agreement we have with Unger to settle alongside their people. I don't have to go along for that." Her fine features grew wistful, and for a moment, she no longer looked quite so young. "I must say that I am getting a bit weary of pools and chairs, and Hyvilma has no convenient bodies of salt water in which to swim." A wry smile lifted her lips. "I imagine I will quite literally be itching for an ocean by the time my duty is through."

Her eyes swept around the table, lighting on each of us in turn. "What about all of you?" she asked. "Assuming there be no war on, what are your plans? Will you go back home, Lieutenant, and take on a new client? Peter, you have school, do you not?"

Peter answered while I was considering my reply. "If we go back right now, I can make the mid-year term." He shrugged broad shoulders. "Again, as you say, if there isn't a war on." He looked over at me.

"Uh…" I began eloquently. "Man, I don't know. How many things have happened in the last set of weeks? I'm just glad everyone's okay." I looked over at Sirena. "I guess we'll have to figure things out when we get back on *Majera*."

Rakotoson emerged through swinging doors trundling a large cloth-draped cart laden with silver dishes, some steaming while others glistened. The odor of fresh meat, flatbread, and spices wafted in with him, and my belly gurgled in anticipation.

"Well, I shall be sorry to miss the next adventure," the princess said. She then flashed a cheerful smile. "But do not fret. As Pinky would say, the only constant is change. And should your course take you past a little blue world named after a friend of yours, know that you will always be welcome in my pool."

I grinned back, thinking of our last "pool party" together on the beach of Sirena in the shadow of the ruined *Émile*.

"We will definitely take you up on that," I said.

Chapter 22

Launch +80

It was nice getting to take a couple of weeks to stretch my legs back on Hyvilma, though there was a nervous quality to everything that hadn't been there the last time we'd been planetside. Folks were a little too quick to laugh, or broodingly silent. Waiting for the other shoe to drop, I guess.

Things were better at the hostel we stayed at next town over. To hear the old trio who ran the place tell it, they hadn't even known a rebellion had gone on. We let the matter lie. Politics was the job of the commission. We were just there to hike and sight-see while the *Majera* got fixed.

Majera. I was dying to get back on *Majera* again. It was like the opposite of claustrophobia. Agoraphobia? No, that wasn't quite right. It wasn't that I disliked the outdoors. And given that I'd spent half the last year inside my little ship, you'd think I'd have had enough of it: my little three-meter by three-meter room, the crowded bridge, the narrow wardroom, the odd smells the air system never could quite get out, and not just the ones Pinky produced for comic effect. But I hadn't. It was *my* ship. I found comfort in its defined space, its limited confines. I knew every inch of it, and it had never let me down.

Frankly, I'd balked when Pinky had proposed taking a week off while *Majera* got overhauled. And it had been like pulling a cat off a tree to get Peter away from *Majera*. He'd gotten to the point where he didn't trust anyone fiddling with the ship's innards. But we were beyond jury-rigging things together. We needed new parts, and we needed professional calibration and certification of the new components. That was more than what he could do, and I couldn't make the repairs go any faster by watching over the technicians' shoulders.

More than that, both Pinky and Fareedh had been keen on getting fresh air, and I wasn't about to deny them anything. A couple of times, my thoughts had wandered to the dark place of contemplating the world I'd be in if I'd lost Pinky or Fareedh, or both of them. I'd recoiled very quickly.

Sirena's absence left a hole, too. Her pool/quarters was already being converted back to a workshop, though it really wouldn't be marked as Peter's domain until he turned it into the ordered chaos that was his preferred environment.

So I also avoided thinking about that. I had gotten really good at that, lately — not thinking about things. Like the can of glitter balls that had gotten opened when I'd kissed Marta. I definitely wasn't going to think about that.

Even if it was really hard.

I hugged my knees and looked into the brightening indigo at the horizon. It was both strange and comforting to be on a world with a day close to the one we used shipboard. It was funny; I'd grown up on Vatan, with its 51-hour days and endless twilights. We used the 24-hour cycle shipboard, but the days can blur together what with no sunlight to anchor them. On Hyvilma, there was no question when day or night was, and I slipped easily into the primordial rhythm of waking and sleeping with the sun. Hyvilma's rotation was 26 hours, which made everything feel just a little more relaxed and laid back. It helped, especially out here, sitting on what passed for grass, rustling soothingly in the light pre-dawn breeze. For a few minutes, I could let my mind drift.

I'd woken up with a song in my head. Just a pop song that had been popular back on Vatan. I couldn't remember any of the words except the chorus: "Free under the rising suns." I let it become the only thing in my thoughts, almost a mantra. Eventually, I started humming the tune out loud, rocking side to side, not fully aware that I was doing it.

The first rays of the Hyvilman sun crested the far-off hills, filling the shallow valley before me with golden light. The arrow-like trees that ran along the river seemed to catch fire at their tips, the flame quickly running down to the ground. My throat caught at their beauty.

"Aww, don't stop," Pinky's voice came from behind me.

I whirled around on my butt, throwing out a bracing hand to keep from toppling over. He was sitting on the ground, legless, a pink half-egg with arms. He must have been there a while.

"I didn't mean to scare you," he said sheepishly.

"What are you doing there, anyway?" I asked.

He held two arms out rigidly at his side. "Being a scarecrow."

I snorted. "There aren't any birds on Hyvilma."

"See? It worked!"

That merited a bonk on his braincase, not that he had one. I gave him a little smooch on his noggin instead, and he flushed rose.

"Seriously," I said. "What are you doing up so early?"

He shrugged. "What is time to me?"

"Fair enough."

"Anyway, I was playing with my long-range."

"Your…"

"Signal transceiver," he explained. He pantomimed a shape a little bigger than hand-sized and then fiddling with phantom controls. "*Sayars* don't work out here. Plus, it's fun to listen to all the broadcasts. You can pick up unclassified Navy chatter." He tinged pink and quivered a bit. "Sometimes even the scrambled stuff."

I crossed my legs under me and placed my palms on the grass. "Since when have you known how to descramble military signals?"

"That's basic stuff, Kitra!" he said. Then he paused, shading maroon a moment. "Ah, I guess that's new."

"L'éclair?" I asked simply.

"Yup."

"Is it…weird for you? Having him inside of you like that?"

"It's not like that, Kitra. I'm *me*. Anyway, it's fun knowing more stuff. Certainly, he's better off, too."

"Oh? How do you figure?"

"Well, he didn't have much of a sense of humor, and no appreciation at all of fart jokes."

"Great. You're going to be the cause of the next mutiny," I said.

"On the contrary. I'm improving morale. You'll see. Anyway, I've got news."

I shifted to my knees and leaned forward. "Yeah?" The wind tugged at my hair, which I'd taken out of the night's ponytail and forgotten to rebind.

"I'm sure it'll be common knowledge soon enough, but a battleship popped in a few hours ago. Out of Punainen."

I whistled. There were no battleships stationed at Punainen, so it must have come from the First Fleet. I did the mental math — it would have taken two weeks to get here from Sennet, leaving five days before we got back to Hyvilma.

"How did they know what happened?" I asked. "There hasn't been enough time to get word to Sennet and back."

"That's the thing. I don't think they did. Something went down on Sennet. One of the battleships got sabotaged. The Navy put down some kind of plot, but they weren't sure how widespread it was, so they sent the *Vérité* to check out Punainen and Hyvilma. I guess they figured a battleship was big enough to take on whatever got thrown against it."

So the mutiny *had* been all part of a bigger event, like Sirocco had feared. Though, if they only got one ship in the First Fleet, it sounded like it had fizzled before it could get too bad.

"And you got all this from your long-range?"

"Well, most of it. Some of it I already knew." He turned a shade of brownish-pink that was new to me. Maybe new to him, too. "Let's just say Sirocco probably wouldn't be entirely pleased with some of the information I got from her comms officer."

"Oh. Wow." If Pinky was sitting on secret codes and other classified stuff, that was both exciting and scary. Well, at least his stuff would get out of date. Eventually.

"So, it's over?" I asked hopefully.

Pinky spread his arms, all three of them. "Unless it was a trick to get the Navy to split up the First Fleet so someone could take the province. If there's a force big enough to take on the five big ships left at Sennet, then this isn't a rebellion. It's a civil war."

He paused dramatically, just long enough for me to start worrying about my friends on Vatan.

"But Commodore Nazarian doesn't think so. He's the skipper on the *Vérité*," he explained. "I don't think they'd have spared him if they thought Sennet was in danger."

"So it *is* over."

"Probably. More or less. Except for the mop up."

I tugged at a piece of grass. It came out easily in the dewy soil. "What about the commission? You think Nazarian will override it?"

"I doubt it," Pinky said. "After all, things are tied up here, thanks to you."

"Thanks to *us*, you mean."

"That's what I said. 'Us.' Anyway, I imagine Nazarian will want to get back to the rest of the fleet sooner rather than later. It is pretty neat having that big ol' ship here, though. You could even see it before the sun came up. Over there." He pointed at a stretch of lavender sky. I squinted, but if there was anything there, it was lost in the glow.

He thumped the ground with a big fist. "But that's nothing to do with us. The question is, where are we going to go now?"

I blinked. "Go? Um…I hadn't really thought about it. I wanted to see how this all shook out before we made plans." I sighed and ventured unenthusiastically, "I guess we could go back home, if people wanted."

A rustle of footsteps caught my attention. I looked back. Brightly lit in the rising sunlight, Peter, Marta, and Fareedh trotted up the path, hands visoring their eyes.

"I'm all for home," Peter called out. He was in shorts, like me. Fareedh was wearing a dress or a robe, and Marta was in a cute romper.

"Everybody's up early today!" I called back.

Fareedh loped up the grass to get to the summit of my hill. For a moment, he just basked in the new sunlight, arms spread wide, eyes closed. Then he looked at me and said with a smile, "I'm soaking up the rays while I can." I could see the literal truth of the statement on his face—he'd gotten back to his normal deep coloration in the last week. The bones of his face still cast sharper shadows than usual, which alarmed me a bit. He'd been skinny enough as it was.

Peter and Marta joined us at a more leisurely pace, hand in hand, and settled on the grass. Fareedh dropped down, too, and now we made a ragged ring.

Pinky raised a pseudopod, waggling a long finger like a conductor's baton. "I suppose you're wondering why I called you all here today."

"Yes, Mr. Prime Minister?" Marta giggled.

"We're making travel plans, right?" Peter asked. "The ship should be ready in a couple of days."

It seemed like a strange time to have this conversation, before breakfast and all of a sudden. On the other hand, the situation had changed. Might as well make plans.

"Pinky says the revolt fizzled out," I said. "We can pretty much do what we want."

"Great," Peter gusted. "Like I said, when do we go home?"

"Tired of adventure already?" I teased.

He nodded seriously. "Kitra, I've gotten more adventure in the last year than most get in a lifetime. Add to that a mountain of data, on the *Émilie's* hyperspace anomaly and from our wild ride here, not to mention all our other trips. I've got more than enough to start toward my doctorate." He looked at the rest of us in turn. "Don't you all want to go home?"

"I don't," I said. "I feel like…like we're doing something really cool, really special. I don't think I'm ready for it to end." The words tumbled out of my mouth, as if they'd been prepped for days. I guess they had, if only subconsciously.

"Uh, two of us almost died," Peter countered.

"Yeah, I know," I said, looking down.

Pinky piped up, "As a person given a new lease on life, I feel emboldened. We've barely scratched the surface of what there is to find out here. I want to see more."

"Well, I mean, sure, we could always go out again. You know, after school's done," Peter said, without much conviction.

"I think you're missing the elephant in the room," Fareedh said, his low tones soft-edged but compelling. He looked meaningfully at Peter, then at me. I felt my cheeks flush. He was right. We still had some interpersonal stuff to work out.

But that wasn't what was on his mind at all. "Peter, could you skate us into Jump like you did last time?"

He goggled at Fareedh. "Are you serious?"

"Yeah, I'm serious. You told us yourself, 'I'm getting good at this.'"

"That was *one* trip!"

Fareedh leaned to the side, resting a hand on the ground and using the other to gesture. "You and I went over the math backwards and forwards on the way to Hyvilma. Once we had the data, it not only worked, it *had* to work. A Jump into hyperspace with none of the fuel cost of transition."

My mind was buzzing. "Wait a minute. What exactly are you saying?"

"When the pirate ambushed us," Fareedh said, "Peter got us into hyperspace inside the giant's gravity well. It had an unexpected side effect, remember? That's why our tanks are still mostly full." His eyebrow quirked. "I wouldn't think you'd have forgotten a thing like that."

"I didn't exactly forget it. Just, a lot happened since then. So let me get this straight. You're saying we can do it *again*? Like, all the time?"

Fareedh nodded energetically. "Yeah. Based on that last Jump, we learned you can effectively make a bubble of null-dimension that connects you to hyperspace without plunging all the way in. Or you can think of it as extending hyperspace to surround *Majera* rather than inserting the whole ship. The math works out identically either way."

"And...that means less gas used."

"It means virtually *no* gas used."

I rocked back on my heels. The universe seemed to unfurl in front of me, a thousand constellations behind the bright purple sky. This meant that we could Jump *anywhere* without worrying about whether there was a suitable place to refuel nearby or not. The time we'd ended up at Jaiyk without fuel after our first Jump would have been no big deal. How many more new planets and places were there to discover?

"And this is...safe?" I breathed.

He shrugged. "We're here, aren't we?"

I turned to Peter. "And this is safe?" I asked again.

"Well, I mean, maybe we just got lucky."

Fareedh retorted, "C'mon, man. It was pure computation and you know it."

My heart pulsed loudly in my ears. I licked my lips. We could really do it.

Fareedh continued, his dark eyes dancing. "This practically doubles our range, since we don't have to detour for watering holes on the way when we plan our course. Heck—we may not even *have* a three-parsec limit anymore. Plus, we don't have to worry about pirates or rebels or anybody. We can always just run away. The entire Frontier is open. Just think of it!"

Peter swallowed. His eyes seemed to glaze.

"Wait, wait, wait," I interjected, coming to reality. "If you guys are right, then this is going to change the course of history. This is way bigger than just us."

Pinky pulsed yellow. "Right. Don't we have an obligation to share this with everyone?"

Peter's eyes went back into focus. "Yeah. Don't we?"

I looked at Fareedh expectantly. We had a point.

"Short answer, yes. But." Fareedh paused and took a breath. "If we go back right now, it'll take at least two weeks just to get back to Vatan. Then finding the right people to talk to. Then writing up papers."

Marta broke in, "Not to mention patenting the process."

"Right," Fareedh said. "That'll all take time. Months. Maybe years." He smiled a little shyly. "I kinda want to have a little more fun before we go back."

"Fun?" I gasped. "Getting shot and all that?"

He shrugged. "I got better. And you're only young once."

Peter looked unconvinced.

"Again, I'm not saying we shouldn't go back and give this amazing development to the universe," Fareedh said smoothly. "But hey, won't you feel a lot more confident if we've got several trips using this technique under our belts? I'm just saying, wait one more trip." He turned to Peter. "Besides, if we're out another few months, it'll be easier when you get back. It'll be the start of a new academic year. You won't have to try to get in for a mid-year term. And you'll have even more data. A tried and tested technique."

"Well..."

I looked at Marta. The sunlight had turned her wind-blown curls to gold, and she looked like something ethereal. My voice caught before I got it working again. "What do you think, Marta?"

Marta frowned, wrinkles deeply creasing her forehead. "I don't know that I'm ready to go home yet. I'm…still working through a few things." Abruptly, her face cleared. "I'm happy being with the people I love. If we go out again, it'll be that much longer we're all together, with no obligations to anybody but each other." She cast her gaze back to Peter. "I won't make you go if you don't want to. But, I think I do want to."

He swallowed, looked down at his lap, then back at her. "It always comes down to me, doesn't it?" he said at last.

She smiled hopefully at him.

Peter looked at Fareedh. "And we'd do a test Jump first, right? No going out to deep space or a star without fuel right off the bat?"

Fareedh nodded. "Of course."

"And you promise we won't be out for years."

Marta said, "We still have an eight-week limit on supplies."

Pinky added, "And we still use gas for maneuvering."

"And let's face it. The money from Sirena's commission covered repairs, but provisioning for another trip will just about use up what's left," I said. I looked at Peter. "Unless you really want to cash out now and call it a day."

Peter shook his head. "We've never been in this for the money, Kitra. You know that." He was starting to look more comfortable. "So after this last jaunt, we'll go home and tell everyone what we did?"

"Whatever you want," Fareedh said. "We can even put a copy of the log somewhere safe on Hyvilma in case something happens to us out there."

Almost despite himself, as if he was resisting with all his might, a slow grin spread across Peter's face. He looked over at me. "You know, if the universe wanted to do us in, it's sure had plenty of opportunities."

He took to his feet, hands on his hips. "What the hell."

Pinky sprouted legs, rising gently above the ground. "One more trip?" he whooped, thrusting a ragged fist into the air.

Marta sprang up. "Where shall we go?" she sang excitedly.

"Sirena, first, of course," Fareedh said, getting to his feet, "We'll be able to stock up on anything we need. Plus, if we time things right, the princess'll be planetside when we get there."

Pinky pulsed happily at that.

"And then?" Peter asked, offering me a hand. I took it, and he hoisted me up with such strength that it was almost like flying.

"The galaxy is our oyster," I said with a grin. "Let's see just how far we can go!"

About the Series

Back when my father was a kid, they had science fiction books for young adults and kids. They called them "juveniles", and they usually featured a young hero flying to the stars. I grew up on these and loved them.

Over the years, YA became all about dystopia and fantasy. I enjoyed The Hunger Games and Harry Potter as much as everyone else, but I missed the space adventures. I wanted to see stories that weren't zero-sum game fights against a Big Bad, that featured reasonably accurate science and characters who struggled with realistic problems. Tales of friendship, ingenuity, and wonder.

Kitra was my first book. It was more successful than I could have dreamed. Years after it came out, it's still getting glowing reviews. It resonates with people. The found family, the diversity in representation, the "strange new worlds," Pinky's jokes: all of these made readers happy again and again.

But there was one common refrain: people wanted to know more. About Kitra and her ragtag crew. The nature of Pinky. The planets beyond the Frontier.

And so I wrote *Sirena*, and now *Hyvilma*. I hope you enjoy it as much as I enjoyed creating it!

~

The lifeblood of every author is audience feedback. Please consider leaving a review (of whatever length) on Amazon, GoodReads, or your favorite platform.

About the Publisher

Founded in 2019 by Galactic Journey's Gideon Marcus, **Journey Press** publishes the best science fiction, current and classic, with an emphasis on the unusual and the diverse.

Also available from Journey Press:

***Kitra* by Gideon Marcus - A YA Space Adventure**

Stranded in space: no fuel, no way home…and no one coming to help!

Nineteen-year-old Kitra Yilmaz dreams of traveling the galaxy like her Ambassador mother. But soaring in her glider is the closest she can get to touching the stars — until she stakes her inheritance on a salvage Navy spaceship.

***Sirena* by Gideon Marcus - Book 2 in the Kitra Saga**

One starship, six friends, 10,000 lives in the balance.

Young captain-for-hire Kitra Yilmaz has gotten her first contract: escort the mysterious Princess of Atlántida beyond the Frontier and find her a new world. It's a risky job, fraught with the threat of pirates, dangerous squatters, and rising romantic tensions.

***I Want the Stars* by Tom Purdom - A Timeless Classic**

Fleeing a utopian Earth, searching for meaning, Jenorden and his friends take to the stars to save a helpless race from merciless telepathic aliens.

Hugo Finalist Tom Purdom's *I Want the Stars* is one of the first science fiction novels to star a person of color protagonist.

DO YOU WANT TO TRAVEL BACK IN TIME?
WWW.GALACTICJOURNEY.ORG